# THE MYSTERY OF THE DOUBLE DOUBLE CROSS

# THE MYSTERY OF
# THE DOUBLE
# DOUBLE CROSS

## Mary Blount Christian

*Cover and frontispiece* by Marie DeJohn

Albert Whitman & Company, Niles, Illinois

Library of Congress Cataloging in Publication Data

Christian, Mary Blount.
   The mystery of the double double cross.

   Summary: When Jeff volunteers to drive a
limousine for his sick brother, he is kidnapped and
taken to a hideout located directly in the path of
a hurricane.
   [1. Kidnapping—Fiction. 2. Hurricanes—Fiction.
3. Mystery and detective stories] I. De John,
Marie, ill.   II. Title.
PZ7.C4528My            [Fic]            82-2575
ISBN 0-8075-5374-3                     AACR2

*To Beth Carrington*

# CHAPTER ONE

Jeff was startled awake by the tinny sound of his alarm clock ringing.

Blast! he thought to himself. John must have come into his bedroom during the night and set it. Of course he *had* forgotten to tell John that today was a teacher in-service day and there was no school.

He gritted his teeth angrily. Why did his brother have to treat him like an infant? Slipping in to check on him like a mother hen looking after her baby chicks—even checking to see if he'd pulled the tab on his alarm!

Jeff closed his eyes and tried to fall back asleep. It was no use. Finally he rolled from bed with a yawn and a stretch. He might as well get up and have breakfast with John.

Jeff padded down the hall past his brother's room. The door was still closed. Odd, he thought. He heard muffled moaning.

Tapping on the door, he called to his brother. "John? Are you all right?"

"Not really," came the reply.

Jeff opened the door and started toward his brother's bed. He stopped when John waved him back.

"Don't come any closer. I'm sick as all get out. And I don't want you to catch whatever I've got."

"You look awful!" Jeff admitted. "All green, except for the dark circles under your eyes! What is it?"

"My stomach. A virus, I guess. I feel sick enough to die. But I've just got to get up. I can't miss work. Not today, anyway."

Jeff frowned. His brother was twenty-one, only five years older than he. But John had completely taken charge since their parents were killed in the car crash a year ago. He was trying to be both mother and father to Jeff—maybe trying too hard. He'd forgotten how to be a brother.

"I'll fix you some mild tea and toast," Jeff offered. "Maybe that'll make you feel better."

8

John pushed himself to his elbows, wincing. "No, no," he protested. "I'll do it myself. Later."

Ignoring him, Jeff went into the kitchen. "I am old enough to fix a little tea and toast, big brother," he muttered under his breath. "Sometimes I think John is trying to retard my growth! He's a lot tougher on me than Mom or Dad would be."

Jeff felt empty inside at the thought of his parents. He put the kettle on to boil and hurriedly flipped on the radio to break the silence.

"Tropical Storm Bernice was upgraded to Hurricane Bernice during the night," the newscaster said. "The Galveston weather bureau reports that at midnight last night the hurricane was situated at twenty-two degrees north and eighty-four degrees west. That is 730 miles southeast of Galveston. Bernice is moving at twenty miles per hour and building intensity."

"Blast!" Jeff mumbled. "I guess I'd better get in some supplies, just in case. Let's see, some masking tape for the windows—no need to let glass fly around if a window does get broken. And I guess some canned food and bottled water—the electricity could go off, even if we don't get a direct hit. We could pick up enough squalls for that. The storm will probably burn out before it gets here, though. Most do."

Jeff glanced out the kitchen window. The leaves hung dead still on the trees. No wind at all. The sparrows and redbirds pecked hungrily at the seed on the bird feeder. The squirrels frantically dug at their nut stashes. There were no quarrels over territory now.

Jeff knew that generally the wild animals ate their fill early if bad weather was on its way. And there seemed to be an unwritten rule among them—no fighting in an emergency situation.

Were the birds and squirrels behaving politely because they knew a hurricane was coming?

No major hurricane had hit Houston since Carla, around twenty years ago. The old-timers said the city was "ripe for a big one," and they were as smart as the squirrels, Jeff figured.

While the water came to a boil, Jeff checked the batteries in the flashlight and set it on the kitchen cabinet. He pulled the first-aid kit and a few candle stubs from the drawer. Then he scouted for matches.

That done, he poured the hot water into the cup and swished the tea bag around. When the toast popped up, he buttered it lightly.

Jeff took the tray into John's room. His brother sat up. His face paled, and he turned his head away.

"Oh, get that food out of my sight," John

moaned. "I can't stand the smell of it. Call my boss, will you? Tell him to get another driver. Then you'd better hurry. You'll be late for school. Did you have your breakfast?"

Jeff snatched the tray. Even when John is sick he doesn't give up smothering me, he thought. He decided not to remind John about the day off. It would be nice to have a day of freedom without his brother telling him what to do.

Instead, he touched John's forehead. "You're burning with fever. Let me call the doctor," he offered.

"No, you've got to get to school. The virus will probably be gone in twenty-four hours, anyway. Let me rest. I just wish I didn't have to miss work. I hate to lose all that money."

"It wouldn't matter so much if you'd let me go to work, too," Jeff snapped. "I *want* to work, you know."

"Now don't start on me, Jeff," John said, waving him away. "You have a job, and that's to get an education and to live the way a teenager should. Hurry and call my boss. Then get to school, will you? Don't be late."

John pulled the covers over his head in an ob-

11

vious dismissal. Jeff whirled and left the room.

He carried the tray back to the kitchen and scrambled himself an egg. He was steamed over not being allowed to work part-time.

John seemed to feel it was only his responsibility to pay their bills. His alone. Jeff didn't agree. He wanted to work so he could help out. And he wanted to work so he could have some money of his own.

Jeff hated getting an allowance handed out to him. He had to ask John for every extra, just like a little kid. He had to do chores for money to take a girl to the movies. If he had his own—

He was tempted to go back and argue, but he didn't. John was too sick. He didn't need to use his energy arguing.

Jeff knew it was more than just a need for the money that made John want to work today. It was his sense of pride, too. Today was a big day for the limo company where John drove. Today was the meeting of a big oil cartel in Houston.

The limo drivers all wanted to chauffeur the important oil executives. And not just because they tipped big. The job was exciting. Ever since they had gotten to be targets for terrorist groups, the businessmen had started traveling in secret.

12

The limo company even used decoys! One man did nothing but get driven around in a duplicate limousine, just to throw off terrorists and kidnappers.

John didn't know how the decisions were made about who was to drive whom. He thought that Ray, his boss, probably decided by drawing names out of a hat, or maybe just by his own whim. All the drivers were treated fairly, though, and got their big chances pretty regularly.

A shiver shot up Jeff's spine. It all seemed so mysterious and dangerous—cloak and dagger stuff. He finished his egg and toast and glanced at his watch. Someone should be at the limo service switchboard by now, he figured. He'd better call so they could get another driver for the cartel meeting today.

Too bad, Jeff thought. John would've loved driving a big oil executive around. He still talked about driving the Rolling Stones when they were in town for a concert last year. That had to be just as tricky, with all those fans chasing after them!

Jeff dialed the first three digits of the limo company's number. He hesitated. Wait a minute, he told himself. He and John really did need the income. The money their parents had left was hardly enough. A leaky roof could wipe out their savings.

Besides, this would show John just how responsible his younger brother really was. After all, Jeff told himself, he had had his own driver's license since his sixteenth birthday a few months ago. He'd gotten it over John's protests, of course. He'd practiced a lot since then, under John's watchful and critical eye.

And he'd listened for hours to John talking about his job. What to do. What to say. And when to keep quiet, too. Jeff figured he knew everything about driving the limo he needed to know. And he knew the city as well as he knew his way to school.

Jeff returned the phone to its cradle. He'd decided. He would drive the executive around today. John didn't have to know until the day was over, anyway. And neither did the limo service, if Jeff played his role right.

He was just filling in for his big brother. What harm could come of it?

# CHAPTER TWO

John's dove gray chauffeur's uniform hung on the bathroom door, ready to be steamed wrinkle-free by the hot mist from his morning shower.

Jeff showered, then slipped into the uniform and stood before the full-length mirror, trying to be honest about how he looked. He was grateful he'd grown tall early.

The uniform was a little loose and a little long on him. But once he was seated with his back to the passenger, who would notice? He pulled the cap bill square over his eyebrows. With his face shadowed by the bill he looked like John, he decided. Well, almost.

Jeff called through John's closed door. "You going to be all right while I'm gone? Can I get you anything?"

"I'll be okay," John replied. "Have a good day at school. If you're going to be late, call me. Hear?"

Jeff stifled the urge to reply, "Yes, Mommy." At least John still hadn't remembered about the teacher in-service day.

Now all Jeff had to fool were the limo people and the oil executive—if he drew him, that is.

Jeff drove his fifteen-year-old Chevy—bought over John's "big brother" protests—to the hotel where the limo was quartered. He was glad he had his own transportation.

It would've been a real hassle getting the keys to John's car without explaining too much. Jeff smiled smugly to himself. He'd argued long and hard with John before getting his own car. At last he'd managed to convince John that the poor bus system made getting to and from school chancy at best.

The car Jeff had chosen had had to be towed home from the used car lot. John never believed it could be made to run again. He had thought it would keep Jeff happy and busy, just tinkering with it in the garage. But he had promised to let Jeff keep the car if he could make it run.

Jeff, helped by some of his buddies from auto-mechanics class, had coaxed the old Chevy back to life. Dismayed as John must've been, he had stood by his promise. But he still refused to let Jeff work for the gas and upkeep expenses. John doled out money a little at a time so he could keep control of the car. Jeff was tired of feeling constantly in his debt.

Jeff pulled into the hotel's underground garage and parked. He walked briskly through the connecting tunnel and took the elevator up to the lobby.

Catching a quick, deep breath, Jeff squared his shoulders and walked toward the canopied entrance. He already knew the limo would be parked at one of the spaces out front reserved just for the limo company. That way a hotel security guard could keep an eye on it.

Several other guys in gray uniforms hovered around the limo's service desk in the crowded lobby. A few seemed lost in their textbooks as they waited for driving assignments. The job gave them plenty of time between runs to study for their college courses. Nearly all of them, including John, went to school, although they couldn't take full class loads.

Pulling the cap bill lower over his face, Jeff moved through the automatic doors and scooted past the doorman, who was arguing with a taxi driver who'd parked in the wrong zone. The doorman paid no attention to Jeff.

He stepped past the *Chronicle* and *Post* coin-automated newsstands. Both papers featured the new hurricane kicking up in the Gulf. "Storm Threatens Oil Rigs in Gulf; Crews Evacuated," said one headline. "Craft Warnings Posted as Precaution," said the other.

"I'll do the storm shopping before I pick up my passenger," Jeff thought. "I can stash supplies in the trunk of the limo and transfer them to my car later."

He glanced around him as he reached the limo. No one seemed to pay any attention to him. He knew the security guard was somewhere close by. But he wouldn't say anything unless someone tampered with the limo. And it was dove gray uniforms, not familiar faces, the guard looked for.

Jeff opened the door and pulled down the sun visor. The keys were there, just as John had once told him.

So far, so good.

# CHAPTER THREE

Jeff knew exactly what to do. He'd eagerly listened to his brother many times as he talked about his job. He'd never realized all that knowledge would come in so handy.

He flipped on the two-way radio. "John here," he said, trying to make his voice just a little deeper than usual. "What's the gig? Over."

"Ray here," the reply came. "You're to be at Intercontinental passenger pickup, Blue Terminal, 10:45."

"Right," Jeff replied. "Do I get the brass ring?" He used the expression he'd heard John use.

"You know I can't tell you that yet, John," Ray said. "Just be there. On time."

"John out," Jeff said. Of course he knew Ray wouldn't tell him if he was to drive an executive or a decoy. Not yet, anyway. The security rules for hauling VIPs were strict. They'd been planned long ago, ever since executives in foreign countries had begun to attract terrorists and kidnappers.

The limo company had worked it out so the driver didn't know anything ahead of time. That way he couldn't say anything that might tip someone off. He couldn't be "bought," either.

It sounded exciting and mysterious—and dangerous. John had told Jeff about some drivers in foreign countries. They had been killed right on the spot when their passengers had been kidnapped. They were of no importance to the terrorists. The drivers had only been in the way.

But there were so many good things about the limo job—earning good money, meeting important and exciting people, being a small part of the big events in Houston. John had stressed those more to Jeff. And when Jeff worried about his big brother's safety, John laughed at him.

"Just see that the newspapers spell my name right," he had once said, teasing Jeff. "It'll be my last chance to make the headlines, and I want my name to be accurate."

Jeff turned onto the freeway loop and flipped on the FM news and music station. He might as well enjoy some music on the long drive to the Intercontinental Airport.

"...gusts to 130 miles an hour and increasing," the announcer was saying. "The Galveston Weather Bureau reports that Hurricane Bernice is now moving north, northwest at twenty-five miles per hour. Meteorologists still are not predicting where landfall might be, or when. They have issued a Hurricane Watch for the Gulf Coast from Brownsville, Texas, to Gulfport, Mississippi."

Three coastal states. The watch covered a lot of territory, Jeff thought. At least it was only a watch, not a warning. A watch meant people should stay ready, just in case a hurricane hit. A warning meant the hurricane was on its way and people should seek shelter.

A warning was usually given twelve hours or less before the earliest parts of a storm hit land, he remembered. There was plenty of time to worry. But what had the announcer said earlier this morning? At midnight the storm had been seven hundred thirty miles southeast of Galveston? If Bernice kept up that speed, landfall could occur in twenty hours or less. Speeds varied, and storms were erratic, of course. This one could slow down or die out altogether.

Jeff brushed away his anxiety. A warning would give him plenty of time to worry. He'd be home, safe and sound, before the weather people even knew what Bernice was going to do. It might even hit somewhere else, in another state.

He glanced at some of the oaks and cottonwood trees that bordered the feeder lane of the 610 Loop. The leaves rustled lightly. "Four-to-seven-mile gusts here," he thought, pleased that he remembered the wind chart from his aviation ground-school class. Maybe he could get a little practical experience with all that stuff he was learning at the magnet school.

John had argued that Jeff shouldn't travel halfway across Houston twice a day for the special classes in aviation. Jeff remembered with some satisfaction that he'd finally won that argument, at least.

Moving north on I-45, he passed Northline Shopping Center. The traffic here was fierce, as usual. But the limo handled like a floating cloud. It smelled a little like last night's cigarette smoke, Jeff noticed, but he'd soon take care of that. He smugly remembered the routine.

Before he reached the Intercontinental Airport turnoff, Jeff moved onto the feeder lane and pulled into the Kwik-4-U Carwash. The limo company had contracts with that chain all over Houston to wash the limos. The company insisted that its sleek pewter-colored cars be washed and vacuumed immediately before passenger pick-up.

While the limo was quickly washed, vacuumed, and deodorized, Jeff shopped at the Stop 'n' Go Market next door. He bought beans, crackers, apple-sauce, canned juices, bottled water, and canned meats that could be eaten cold.

He signed the charge for the carwash and entered the amount in the logbook he found in the car's glove compartment. He stored the supplies in the trunk.

Jeff sniffed as he opened the limo door. The inside smelled leathery, like a new car fresh off the assembly line at Detroit.

He pulled onto the long stretch of road that passed Greenspoint Mall and a line of offices, restaurants, and motels. He turned up onto the high overpass that seemed almost too narrow for the limo.

The tall pines along John Kennedy Boulevard rustled slightly. A flag flapped against itself. The breeze didn't seem to be steady, though.

Bernice'll never hit here, Jeff thought. It's too quiet. This can't be what it's like before a hurricane.

As he approached the airport, Jeff glanced at the information boards along the drive. Terminal B—follow the blue signs. The dashboard clock showed 10:30 A.M. Good. He'd be at the pickup early enough to beat his passenger, but late enough to avoid attracting too much attention.

He could see there weren't many planes left tied down near the row of privately owned hangars. Their owners probably believed in an ounce of prevention. They'd probably flown them farther inland, to Dallas maybe, or even to Oklahoma. There was no need for him to panic, though. Owners of expensive planes always took early precautions. Their investments were huge. They would rather move their airplanes unnecessarily than lose them to a storm that arrived ahead of schedule.

Jeff pulled the limo under the parking overhang at the passenger pickup. Somewhere inside him a little warning bell sounded. Maybe he'd never get away with this.

He decided to ignore the warning.

The oil executive—if Jeff drew him—would still get his money's worth, wouldn't he? What did it matter who drove him, as long as the guy got where he wanted to go? And who was to know the difference?

Jeff checked the inside temperature gauge. It read 72 degrees. Perfect. He switched the radio to the station with the quiet music. John said unless the passenger suggested something different, the driver was supposed to provide music that was slow and soft.

Jeff chuckled, remembering that John had driven the Rolling Stones around. He could just bet they requested something different, all right.

Jeff felt his pulse quicken as the two-way radio gurgled to life.

"Ray here. You there, John?"

"John here," Jeff answered. "I'm at the pickup point."

"Bingo, John! You get the brass ring."

# CHAPTER FOUR

"You know how it goes, John," Ray said. "The VIP
will give you the route you're to take. He'll tell you
where he wants to go and what time he wants to get
there. He's the boss, hear? Do what he says, even if
you think he's wrong. Okay?"

"Okay," Jeff replied. He could feel his heart
pumping.

"Merle's the decoy driver. But that's not your
problem. You just do your best to keep this guy
happy."

"How will I know him?" Jeff asked. "What's his
name? What's he look like?"

"He'll know you. And if he wants you to know
anything, he'll tell you," Ray said. He laughed. "I

know this security is kind of James Bondish, but it's the way the oil guys want it. And since they're paying the bills, that's the way they'll get it."

Jeff signed off, then sat staring at the automatic doors. Passengers poured out, carrying over-night bags, duffle bags, and four-suiters. He watched for someone with just a briefcase.

He figured the man would be in Houston only for the day, just long enough for the meeting. He'd probably get a return flight in the evening. He wouldn't have luggage, more than likely.

Jeff was right. A man dressed in a dark gray three-piece suit and tightly clutching a briefcase barged through the doors and the crowd. He approached the limo without hesitation. "John Tyler?" he asked.

Jeff got out and snapped open the rear door. At the same time, he reached to relieve the man of the briefcase.

The man snatched it from reach, frowning. Jeff blushed. He saw then that the briefcase was chained to the man's wrist. Of course the executive wouldn't let anyone else handle the case. It probably contained all sorts of secret company information needed for the cartel meeting.

Jeff pushed the lock tab down and slammed the door shut. He got back behind the wheel.

"Turn that music off," the man muttered. "It sounds like a funeral. Has that storm blown itself out yet? I guess you get lots of them that fizzle out, don't you?"

"It's on the move and building," Jeff replied, reaching to turn off the radio. "But we've had worse ones blow out without ever reaching land. I expect this one will, too."

"Umm," the man replied. "Take the Eastex into town, will you?"

"Yessir," Jeff replied. Highway 59, or the Eastex, was a lot bumpier and not as pretty as I-45. Maybe traveling on poor roads was one of the prices a VIP had to pay to avoid being kidnapped. What a life!

Jeff headed around the terminal, past the all-day parking lot, and out onto the boulevard again. He turned left at the light and headed past the Hertz resale lot toward the Eastex.

Jeff turned right on the Eastex, surprised at how easy the limo took the road. A piece of cake! he thought smugly. John should see his little brother now!

He knew he wasn't supposed to talk to the passenger except to answer a question. The man seemed untalkative, anyway, so Jeff concentrated on the traffic. He glanced now and then at the rearview mirror, studying the man's image.

The oilman looked to be in his mid-fifties. He was elegantly dressed, with salt-and-pepper hair. No glasses. Contact lenses, maybe? Jeff wondered. There was nothing too distinguished about him, except his obviously expensive clothes.

Jeff's eyes flicked toward the side mirror. Was anyone following them? That red taxi? That sleek new car? How did television detectives pick out tails from the rest of the traffic?

The man interrupted Jeff's daydream. "There's a public phone in the next block," he said. "Stop there."

For some reason, Jeff's stomach gave a lurch. Was he suddenly scared? Or maybe he was coming down with John's virus? He spotted the blue bell on a white background, the sign for public phones.

Jeff pulled the limo into the parking space. He reached back and flipped up the lock, then jumped out and opened the rear door.

Unexpectedly the man smiled, his first change of

expression since he had gotten into the limo. It struck Jeff as somehow uncharacteristic, although he knew nothing about this person.

The oilman shoved three quarters into Jeff's hand. "Here. Go inside and get yourself a canned drink or something. I won't be long."

Jeff stared at the coins. He thought it might not be a good idea to leave the limo unattended, with the ignition on. But he knew he wasn't supposed to let the air-conditioning go off, either, because the inside of the car would become uncomfortable for the passenger. If he left to get a drink, he would have to leave the car unlocked with the motor running.

He decided he'd better do exactly what the man told him. It was the guy's money, after all. And Ray had told him to do what the customer wanted.

Jeff didn't like leaving the man and the car alone. But, after all, there were cars coming and going on the lot. And there were plenty of cars passing by on the highway. Nobody would try anything with so many people to see them, would they?

The phone was in an outside, open-air booth. Jeff paused before he went inside the convenience store, looking back. He watched the man drop coins into the phone, enough coins for a long-distance call.

Odd. Why had the man waited until now to make a call? Why hadn't he used a phone inside the terminal, instead of waiting to call from outside, in the famous Houston humidity?

Jeff shrugged off his concern and went into the little convenience store. He ordered a cold grape drink. He glanced back through the plate-glass window. He could see the man still talking on the phone.

Jeff finished his drink and glanced back again. The man was no longer in the booth.

Jeff tossed the can into the plastic container by the door and hurried toward the limo. Through the smoke-glazed car windows, he could see the passenger seated in the backseat.

He trotted past the rusted pickup truck parked nearby and flung open the door to the limo. Jeff slid behind the wheel. "Sorry, sir," he apologized. "I hope I didn't keep you waiting."

He glanced into the rearview mirror when the man didn't say anything. Jeff could see the man shake his head no.

Jeff thought he detected a tenseness about the oilman's jawline that hadn't been there before. Had the phone call been upsetting, maybe? Or was something else bothering him?

Jeff pulled the gear into drive and flipped on the turn signal. He prepared to pull back onto the Eastex.

He glanced into the rearview mirror one more time.

Jeff felt his heart skip a beat as he caught the reflection of a second face.

The hair on the back of his neck prickled as a cool metal cylinder was pressed to the base of his skull.

He heard a distinct click.

# CHAPTER FIVE

"That bullet chamber was empty," the man holding the gun said. His voice was strained, his words, sharp. "The others aren't. So just drive in toward town and connect to the Gulf Freeway."

Jeff gripped the steering wheel so tightly, he could feel his fingers growing stiff and cold. He wanted to do what the man asked. But he felt so quivery he was afraid he might alarm him and make him pull the trigger.

Jeff swallowed hard, trying to get the lump from his throat. It didn't work. "Yes, sir," he said. Cold sweat beaded his lip.

Obediently he drove toward town. Against the dark clouds scudding across the smokey mustard sky, Houston's tall buildings looked like tombstones.

The traffic was awful. At the Loop Jeff cut over

to I-45 again. He wanted to keep moving. He didn't want to give the gunman an excuse to shoot.

He passed the towering Texas Commerce Tower, the Tenneco, and the Spindletop. He circled around Allen Center to join the Gulf Freeway.

What could he do? How could he stop this crazy guy in the backseat from killing him?

The limo eased past the University of Houston cutoff. John must turn there every night on his way to pre-law classes. If only John were here—he'd know what to do!

Jeff's mind flipflopped and spun dizzily with thoughts of desperate escapes. The radio—if he could just key in the two-way radio and lead the conversation. Maybe Ray would catch on and get the police.

Jeff shifted slightly in the seat. He tried to casually stretch his arm toward the radio without the man with the gun seeing him. His fingers were just inches away from the switch.

"I wouldn't do that, if I were you," the man said. "You don't want to upset me and wind up dead now, would you?"

Jeff put both hands back on the wheel. "I don't want to wind up dead anywhere," he replied, trying to keep his voice steady. "But I guess if I'm going to die, the place won't much matter."

The oilman spoke up. "Just do as he says, please."

"Yessir," Jeff said. He figured every minute he wasn't shot had to be in his favor. He would have to cooperate and wait for his chance.

"Get off the freeway here," the man instructed.

Jeff pulled into the parking lot at the Gulfgate Shopping Center. It was jammed with shoppers' cars.

If only people weren't so involved with their own business, Jeff thought, maybe someone would notice what was going on. Maybe he could give some kind of signal. But it was probably too much to expect busy city dwellers to get involved in a kidnapping, especially when they were worried about a hurricane.

"Over there," the man said, pointing to an empty space next to a white van. "Pull in and park."

Jeff pulled into the space and shut off the motor. Where were the shopping center's security patrols when he needed them? he wondered bitterly.

"Now, out!" The man waved his gun.

The three of them got out on the passenger's side, next to the van. As Jeff slid by the radio he managed to key the mike. Ray would eventually notice the radio was on.

Maybe somehow the limo company would track down its car. Grimly Jeff realized that by then it might be too late to save himself and the oilman.

The gunman tapped on the side of the white van. Its door slipped open with a metallic snap. A second man hopped from the van.

"It's about time you got here, Nick!" the second man growled. "What's *he* doing here?" He pointed at Jeff.

"You knew there was a driver," the first man snapped. "Was I supposed to get rid of him while we were on the Eastex? Besides, he can drive."

The second man shrugged. He held a couple of Civil Defense decals. He pressed them onto the van doors.

"Grossmark here goes in the back with me," the man called Nick said. He nodded toward Jeff. "You drive. Terry will be up front with you—to see you behave and don't do nothing foolish."

The second man, the one called Terry, shoved Jeff into the driver's seat, then climbed in on the passenger side.

Jeff pulled out of the parking lot and reentered

the freeway's feeder street. He inched along behind the line of traffic. He tried to think.

All the details seemed to be worked out. These guys knew the VIP's name, even though Jeff himself hadn't known it until now. They had really done their homework. Grossmark, was it? Grossmark. Okay. A guy ought to know who he's risking his life for.

Jeff glanced toward the man beside him, waiting for instructions.

"Head for Galveston," Terry told Jeff. "And no funny stuff."

Jeff gasped. "Galveston! But the storm is probably heading that way. They'll be calling for an evacuation soon, if they haven't already. They'll probably close the bridge by tonight."

Terry grinned at him. "You catch on fast, stupid. We didn't plan on this hurricane scare, but now that it's here, we're going to take advantage of it. Galveston will be the perfect place to hide out. And I got hold of these Civil Defense decals and stuck them on the van so nobody's going to wonder why we're going to Galveston instead of coming from it. Why, we look like regular angels of mercy." He burst into a sinister laugh that sent chills through Jeff.

Jeff glanced over the center rail toward the inbound lanes. They were lined bumper to bumper with station wagons, cars, and vans filled with kids, animals, and television sets and pulling boats of every size and description.

The evacuation was already under way, even if it wasn't official yet.

Jeff knew he was headed into what might be the worst hurricane of the decade. And, if Bernice didn't get him, these guys with the guns probably would.

And nobody, not even his own brother, knew he was missing.

# CHAPTER SIX

The familiar scenes in the fifty miles from Houston to Galveston sped past Jeff's eyes as ideas, wild, hairbrain ideas, ran through his head.

How could he get someone's attention? How could he let someone know that he and the oilman called Grossmark were in trouble—big trouble?

The van's signal lights—what if he turned on the blinkers? Would anyone notice? Or even care, for that matter? What if he went over the speed limit? Would some alert cop flag the van down? Or would the cop just see the Civil Defense stickers and let them go through?

What would happen, he wondered, if he just crashed the van into one of the ramp railings? Jeff thought of one idea after the next. None of them were any good. The gun being held on him was too real. Whatever he tried he'd never get away with. Not alive, anyway.

A barrage of smoke-gray clouds swirled overhead. The weather was definitely getting worse. Jeff realized at least some effects of the hurricane would be felt here whether or not Bernice hit Galveston full force. The side effects of a hurricane could cause some of its worst damage. A storm hitting far south—at Brownsville, maybe—could cause severe floods, squawls, and even tornadoes in the Galveston area.

Jeff drove past Texas City on the left, then Bayou Vista on the right. Already high foamy waves slapped at the boat slips built beneath the houses on the bay.

The palm trees swayed in almost an arc now. Jeff figured the winds were between nineteen and twenty-four miles per hour, which was only a fresh breeze on the wind charts.

He pulled onto the causeway, a mast-high ribbon of concrete that lifted up over the water and connected Galveston Island with mainland Texas.

Mist clouded his view through the windshield. The first rain was here. He switched on the wipers.

"This is crazy," Jeff muttered. "That storm will blow us right off the island."

Terry waved his pistol at Jeff. "It's just an isolated squawl, probably. Shut up and do as you're told. Or you won't have to worry about anything, much less the storm."

To their right, yachts, small fishing boats, and shrimpers lined up in the narrow channel that crossed under the causeway. They were headed for the calmer waters of the bay and the rivers that emptied into it.

Of course there were still some heartier fishermen, their boats buffeted by the rising wind, trying to take advantage of the weather to catch the red fish that ran in the rougher waters. Already the water was an ugly brown from the silt stirred up.

To Jeff's right, thunderhead clouds looked like a stampede across the sky, and they were headed straight inland. The air looked thick with rain out over the Gulf.

Waves dashed the pillars supporting the causeway. By evening authorities would probably have to close it. Three-to-five-foot tides were enough to cover its lowest sections.

Jeff knew that a hurricane could cause surges, or ocean swells, as far as six hundred miles from its center. There would probably be heavy flooding here, even if Bernice missed Galveston. People, animals, even reptiles, would have to seek higher ground. He remembered how a flood last year had driven a big rattlesnake to the back porch at home.

Water could be pushed inland for miles. Even

Texas City across the bay would have to be evacuated. Galveston could be cut off from the mainland. He—and Mr. Grossmark—would be trapped in the island city with the kidnappers. And it was Grossmark who was valuable, not Jeff Tyler, he reminded himself.

The rain now drummed heavily on the van's roof. The man called Terry directed Jeff off the freeway and onto Sixty-first Street.

Flags above the shops that dotted the street were fully extended in the increasing wind. Only instead of the familiar faded blue bait signs, the bending masts supported black rectangles bordered with red. They were hurricane flags.

"You know Stewart Road?" Terry asked.

Jeff nodded. Before their parents died, he and John used to take Stewart Road to West Beach all the time. Now that John was head of the family, though, he said the undertows on West Beach were too dangerous and there weren't enough lifeguards.

"West Beach is the worst possible place to be in any storm, much less a hurricane," Jeff protested. "There's no seawall down that far, just the sand dunes. And they won't hold up long against the wind and tide. We'll be torn to bits by the storm!"

42

# CHAPTER SEVEN

Ignoring Jeff's protests, Terry directed him to drive onto one of the dozens of crushed shell roads that connected to the beach and the houses there.

Jeff glanced about as he pushed the van against the heavy wind. A convenience store with a gas pump on the left, a shell shop and a few scattered houses on the right. Probably all abandoned for the storm. He wanted to remember them.

Just knowing where they were might help later— if he could get away.

The beginning swell had already made the beach much narrower than usual. The waves looked overwhelming—not at all like the rollicking happy ones that usually licked at the shore. These waves were farther apart, too, which was a sure sign that the island would be flooded, even if the center of the hurricane didn't strike here.

Through the almost blinding rain, Jeff could see the blinking yellow lights of the buoys that warned big ships to come no closer to shore.

"That brown house!" Terry yelled. "The shingled one. Turn in there."

A large antenna, too large to be a TV antenna, was bolted to the east side of the house that Terry pointed out. It had to mean there was a ham radio inside. Jeff's hopes quickened. He knew all about ham radios from his communications class. If only—

"Park under the house," Terry commanded.

Jeff pulled next to the red compact car under the house and shut off the van motor. He could feel his knees trembling even though he was still seated. He was stiff with tension, tension from driving on the rain-slicked roads and tension from the constant threat of Terry's gun. His foot on the gas pedal was completely numb. He was sure he couldn't run for it, even if he had the chance.

A sudden gust of wind shook the van violently. Sand peppered it.

"Out," Terry said.

Jeff pushed against the door until it gave way. Sand and salt stung his face. The wind whistled through the fragile dune grass and swept rain up under the house.

Jeff shivered. His uniform felt damp and clingy against his skin.

"Up those stairs," Terry ordered, ripping the decals from the van doors.

Jeff headed up. There was nothing else to do. He could feel the gun barrel against the small of his back. He paused on the porch at the top of the stairs.

A surfboard, waxed and shiny, leaned casually against the porch railing, bumping in the wind. A hand-painted sign that read "Sunny Daze" had jarred loose on one end and now creaked violently on one small nail.

The door suddenly flung open. Another man appeared.

"Get in!" he shouted. "Hurry!"

Jeff felt the flimsily constructed house tremble in the wind. It creaked and groaned on its cranelike legs.

He stood glumly staring about a large room. He was in a typical beach house, with all the furniture, walls, and floors wipe-clean and drip-dry. A short-wave radio was set up in one corner.

Like most of the houses in the area, this one looked too new to have withstood the test of a hurricane. Beach houses weren't built to last, anyway. Insuring them against storm damage was much too expensive, so owners built vacation homes as cheaply as possible, almost expecting them to be destroyed in a bad storm.

Terry shoved Jeff into a lacquered wicker captain's chair. Jeff felt his pulse throbbing in his temples as he obediently sat down.

For the first time, Jeff noticed another person in the room. Standing at the small stove, frying bacon, was a girl about his own age. She was barefoot. A hot pink bathing suit protruded beneath the short poplin jacket she wore zipped to her chin.

What was she doing, mixed up in this mess? Jeff wondered. He felt a moment of blind rage, as if he'd been betrayed by one of his own friends.

Slowly the girl turned her head until their eyes met. There was a dried trickle of blood at the corner of her mouth, as if she'd been struck hard. Her face mirrored terror—no, Jeff decided, worse. Hopelessness.

Jeff knew then. She, too, was caught in the middle. Somehow she'd become a victim just as he was.

Now there were two lives with no one to bargain for them.

# CHAPTER EIGHT

"Hurry with that food!" the third man yelled at the girl. "With this wind the electric power ain't gonna last forever."

Jeff studied the man. He wanted to memorize all the kidnappers' faces. This man's face would be particularly easy to remember. He had a scar on his left cheek and his left earlobe was missing. He looked like a duelist who'd gotten careless once too often.

The man had a cruel, hard expression. It would be easy for him to pull a trigger, Jeff thought.

He glanced at the girl. Her knuckles were white, she was gripping the fork so hard. He could see the muscle in her neck pulsating as she turned the frying bacon.

"Look for some candles," Terry commanded Nick. "And matches, too. Check the food supplies. We need enough to hold out, okay? We could be here a while."

The third man grinned, deepening his scar. "The

house came supplied. Girlie here and her folks believe in plenty of food.''

''Don't call me Girlie,'' the girl mumbled through her clenched teeth. ''And you'd better let me go. When my folks don't hear from me—''

''Just shut up and cook, will you?'' the man with the scar grumbled. ''I didn't know this thing was gonna turn into a blinkin' kiddie camp.''

Mr. Grossmark sat stiffly in one of the wicker chairs. His chained briefcase lay on his lap. He looked tense and worried.

''Let them go,'' he said. ''They can't do anything. By the time they—''

''You got to be kidding!'' Terry interrupted. ''They know too much.''

''Plug in the portable radio,'' Mr. Grossmark suddenly ordered. ''Please,'' he added, glancing nervously about. ''We should find out about the storm, don't you think?''

Jeff was surprised to see that Terry did as he was told. But of course the kidnappers probably wanted the radio on, anyway. They'd want to find out about the storm even more than Mr. Grossmark did.

Terry turned on the portable radio that was on the counter by the stove. It wheezed and whistled and came to life. But only for a moment. The lights in the room suddenly flickered and then went off. At the same time the radio went dead.

The heavy squawl had knocked out the electricity. Maybe the storm band would pass, but that didn't mean the lights or the radio would come back on.

There was a loud crash as something twisted and slammed into the side window. Rain and sand whipped into the room. Glass blew about in stinging slivers.

The girl screamed as glass slivers bombarded her bare legs. Jeff dived for her, shoving her to the floor. He flung himself over her, protecting her from the debris that whirled about the room.

"Shove that big cabinet against the hole!" Terry shouted. "And get those candles lit. Don't either of you turkeys move again, or I'll shoot at the sound!"

Through the broken glass, Jeff could see the large antenna, awkwardly bent. It had crashed into the window. Shortly the two men had shoved a tall metal cabinet into place in front of the gaping hole. But the cabinet didn't stop the cold mist from penetrating the house. Terry lit the candles. The room glowed eerily.

Jeff pulled the girl to her feet. She smiled at him for a fleeting second.

He whirled to Terry. "If the wind gusts are strong enough to twist that antenna, they're already at gale force," Jeff said. "Things are getting worse. Please let us go. We won't tell. We prom—"

"Shut up and sit down," Terry said. "Who'd have thought that a stupid storm—at least the antenna is still connected. The ham radio ought to work."

How could the ham radio work with the electricity off? Jeff wondered. Maybe there was a gas generator. That was it—the radio operated off a gas generator, independent of electricity. They'd probably chosen this house for that very reason. Any storm could cause a power failure, and these guys would have to be able to communicate with the outside.

Jeff glanced at Mr. Grossmark, still motionless in the same chair. In all the confusion over the broken window, he could've started a ruckus, maybe slammed Terry or Nick with his heavy briefcase. But he hadn't. He seemed to be in a kind of stupor.

Well, some guys didn't react well in a crisis, Jeff knew. Some just fell apart. Others waited for someone else to tell them what to do. Maybe Mr. Grossmark was one of those who waited. But a few minutes ago, when he had been ordering Terry to turn on the radio, he had been acting like a leader. Why had he suddenly changed? After all, he was a big executive in an oil company. He should be used to taking action.

"The causeway will close in a few hours," Terry said. "If we're going to do it, now's the time."

"Do it" sounded ominous—final. Jeff held his breath and glanced over at the girl. She looked as scared as he felt.

Terry tied Mr. Grossmark into a chair. The third man brought out an instant camera. He probably wanted proof that Grossmark was alive and well worth the ransom money, Jeff figured.

"Wait a minute," Terry said. "I got an idea." He handed Jeff a rifle.

"Don't worry, Tyler. It's empty. Stand over by Grossmark and point the gun at him."

"But why?" Jeff demanded. "Why should I?"

"So I won't kill you and the girl," Terry said. Meekly Jeff did as they told him. There were three guys there, all of them armed. There was no way he could overpower them with an empty rifle.

The room filled with light as the flash camera fired. Terry took four or five pictures. He stood waiting for the instant pictures to develop.

In a few minutes he grinned. "You take a good picture, kid—John, is it?" He shoved one of the pictures toward Jeff.

Jeff felt a wave of nausea sweep over him. He was suddenly getting the idea. The picture made it look as if *he* were holding Mr. Grossmark hostage. But what was Terry going to do with those pictures? And who would believe anything that crazy, anyway?

"Get those pictures to the mainland before the causeway closes," Terry ordered the man with the scar. "One each for the television stations and for the daily papers. Got it?"

The man nodded. He slipped into rain gear and tucked the pictures into his pocket. Cold biting wind swept in as he opened the door.

Terry waved the gun at Jeff and yelled, "Help me shut this door. And don't try anything."

Jeff did as he was told. The time wasn't right for an escape attempt—not yet. At least, one of the kidnappers was gone now, the one he was most afraid of. And it would take the man the better part of five hours to make it to Houston.

Now there were only two men with guns. And there were three prisoners.

Terry took the ropes off Mr. Grossmark. Jeff felt even better.

But who was he kidding? Three unarmed people against two men with guns was no contest at all. And Jeff wasn't sure if he could count on Mr. Grossmark to do anything at all, not after his earlier performance.

Jeff felt sick with disappointment when Terry used the rope to bind his and the girl's hands. Now Mr. Grossmark was the only prisoner who was free. The oilman sat quietly, staring out the window.

That was odd. Why didn't Terry and Nick tie up Grossmark, anyway? Even if he didn't seem to be the type to fight back, how could the kidnappers trust that he wouldn't try to escape? What was going on?

There was only one thing Jeff was sure about—this house wouldn't make it through a hurricane. Already it shook and creaked. And right now Bernice was still only a moderate storm, with wind gusts of maybe thirty-eight miles an hour. He remembered old-timers saying that Hurricane Carla had had gusts up to two hundred miles an hour.

Jeff knew he had to make a move soon, even if he did it alone, without Grossmark or the girl.

But when? And how?

# CHAPTER NINE

"Can't we use the ham radio to find out about the storm?" Jeff asked. "It obviously runs off a generator."

"Smart kid," said Terry. "You'd like that. You'd like to get the cops down on us. No way! What if some snoop was listening in on our conversation? What if someone put two and two together?" Terry grinned at him. "We'll know if the storm hits, if that's what's bothering you. Won't we?"

Jeff frowned, remembering Terry's concern for the antenna earlier. Why did he care about the antenna if he didn't plan to use the ham radio? He must be planning to use it some time.

The girl shrugged slightly. "Look, my little portable radio is convertible. It has batteries. Pull the plug but leave it turned on."

Terry pulled the plug from the wall and the radio came on in an instant. He turned the volume higher so the news could be heard above the mournful howling wind.

The announcer predicted the causeway to Galveston would close in a few hours. The coordinates showed Bernice increasing to powerful proportions. The weather experts figured it could be the worst hurricane to hit shore in several decades.

A reconnaissance plane was to fly through Bernice in a few hours, the announcer continued. Then the weather bureau would release more details about the size of the eye and the latest information about the storm's direction and rate of speed.

Although Hurricane Carla had struck before Jeff was born, he'd often heard his parents talk about it. People talked about Houston in terms of "B.C." and "A.C."—before Carla and after Carla. He'd seen pictures of mangled and twisted buildings, of cars perched on top of telephone poles.

"Old-timers are laying odds that Bernice will follow the path of Carla," the announcer said.

Jeff knew that information about the eye—the calm center of the storm—was critical. If the eye was small and tight, winds circling it would be extremely fast. The damage caused by the hurricane could be even worse than that caused by Carla. If the eye was large, even more human lives could be lost. Maybe sixty percent of the people in the area had never experienced a hurricane. When the eye passed over, they might think the storm was over and go outside. Then they could be caught by the other side of Bernice.

"Everyone should leave low-lying areas and seek the safety of the mainland buildings opened as shelters by the Red Cross," the announcer said.

"Only a few police will stay on the island of Galveston to curb looting and to protect members of the weather bureau and those few who refuse to leave their homes. Everyone who is staying should alert the authorities."

Don't I wish I could, Jeff thought bitterly.

He glanced through the thick sheets of rain that slammed against the window. The water was rising fast. Angry whitecaps boiled and churned, carrying with them seaweed and sand, ripped from the Gulf floor.

"And now this other news," the announcer said. "Martin Grossmark, president of MG Oil Company, is the apparent victim of a kidnapping.

"MG board members became concerned when Grossmark failed to show up at an important meeting this morning. The oil executive was last seen entering a hired limousine at Houston Intercontinental Airport. The limo was first believed to be driven by LimCo driver John Tyler.

"However, when police went to the Tyler home, they found John Tyler there, home with a viral infection. Identity of the kidnapper is unknown at this time."

Jeff glanced slowly around the room. Every eye was on him. He knew everyone wondered just who he was. He was almost glad his hands were bound and behind his back. At least the kidnappers couldn't see them trembling.

"In this related story just in from News Central, East Texas landowners have filed a class action suit, seeking an injunction against MGC. In the suit, filed this morning in district court, the landowners dispute the oil company's drilling rights. Landowners say that MGC never legally leased land now being drilled on. They claim that the oil company owes them large sums of money.

"MGC president Martin Grossmark was enroute to a meeting with his board to produce the leases in question when he was apparently kidnapped."

Jeff studied the faces around him. Were they still wondering about him? Or were they, like him, now wondering about the lawsuit?

What a coincidence that the president of an oil company was kidnapped at the same time his company was being sued! Martin Grossmark must be under awful pressure. Maybe that was why he seemed to be in a daze.

The radio announcer continued. "The abandoned limousine was discovered late this afternoon in the parking lot of Gulfgate Shopping Center. Police found enough supplies in the trunk to enable the kidnapper to hold out for a considerable length of time. They are not certain why he apparently switched vehicles."

Jeff felt the blood suddenly rush to his head. The cops thought his storm supplies were some kind of preparation for the kidnapping! Why didn't they realize that today half the trunks in Houston had hurricane supplies in them?

Terry grinned at Jeff. "Just wait 'til those pictures get delivered to the papers and television stations with you holding Martin here hostage. They won't have any doubts at all then, will they? The heat will be off us and smack on you."

For an uncertain moment Jeff almost believed Terry. But surely nobody would suspect him—not for long, anyway.

Terry laughed, apparently enjoying Jeff's predicament. "Besides, if you aren't John Tyler, maybe you had your own little deal going. Too bad. Maybe we just came along and stole your thunder, huh?"

"I, I—" Jeff protested weakly.

Nick snickered. "Why, boy, if you escape, they'll probably shoot you on sight!"

# CHAPTER TEN

The food cooked earlier had been ruined when the rain, sand, and glass whipped through the beach house. There was no electricity left for the stove—for some reason the generator fed only the ham radio. Terry opened cans of beans. He untied the girl and let her eat. When she was finished, he tied her up again and untied Jeff.

As Jeff ate, he tried to think up escape plans. He hoped the girl and the oilman were thinking, too. The two kidnappers watched him warily. After hearing the news story on the radio, they probably wondered if he really was another kidnapper. Jeff hoped somehow that suspicion would work in his favor.

"Please let me change clothes," the girl said suddenly. "I'm cold in this bathing suit. Just let me slip on some jeans."

Jeff glanced at her legs. They were covered with goosebumps. She really looked miserable.

"No," Terry replied. He grinned as if he enjoyed making people suffer.

"Let her change!" the oilman snapped. "We're here for a while and this is her house."

Jeff wondered if he'd missed part of the conversation. Or was it just a wild guess on the oilman's part that this house belonged to the girl?

And why was Martin Grossmark again barking commands? Why should Terry do what his kidnap victim ordered?

To Jeff's surprise, Terry untied the girl.

"You've got five minutes in the bathroom," he warned. "If you aren't out by then, I'm coming in after you. And don't try anything cute, hear?"

Jeff hesitated. "When she gets out, may—"

Terry glanced at the oilman before he answered in a growl. "I feel like a nanny in a nursery school! Yeah, yeah, okay. As soon as she's back in ropes."

The girl returned and obediently allowed herself to be rebound. Terry released Jeff. "Like I told her. Five minutes and no funny stuff."

Jeff paused only briefly when he walked through the adjoining bedroom to the bathroom. The bedroom was sparsely furnished. There were windows on two sides, and they rattled ominously from the wind.

Escape was either through the front door, guarded by the men, or out a bedroom window, with an eight-to-twelve foot drop, at least, to the beach. That was how high this house, like most of the other houses on the beach, sat on its pillars.

In the bathroom Jeff noticed a small closet and pulled open the door. Inside were stored scuba gear and life vests. Was it possible this tiny bit of knowledge might come in handy? he wondered.

He returned to the room and his bindings. He just didn't have a plan.

While Terry tied him up again, Jeff watched Mr. Grossmark. The oilman stared gloomily toward the radio, apparently listening to reports of the approaching storm. He must be thinking the hurricane would make it impossible to escape, Jeff thought. The kidnappers knew it was impossible. Maybe that was why they didn't get excited when Grossmark ordered them to let Jeff and the girl use the bathroom.

And maybe that was why they didn't bother to tie the oilman up. Yet it still seemed odd to Jeff. It was as if the kidnappers had some strange hold on Grossmark, as if they knew he wouldn't even try to get away. Could they be threatening someone in his family? Maybe his wife and children had been kidnapped, too, and were going to be harmed if Grossmark didn't cooperate.

Jeff was tired of trying to figure things out. He was exhausted. He could see by the lighted dial on Mr. Grossmark's watch that it was almost six o'clock. They had been sitting in this beach house all afternoon. He knew the girl must feel tired, too. Her eyes were darkly circled. His own eyes felt grainy and swollen. He could hardly keep them open.

Jeff's head nodded. The next thing he knew, Terry was untying his ropes. He led Jeff and the girl into the small bedroom. He tied them into straight chairs.

The room was on the leeward side of the house, sheltered from the approaching storm. Here the growing wind sounded more like a dull roar.

Terry tugged at Jeff's ropes, then stood back as if studying his face. "Who are you, anyway, kid?" he asked. He shrugged. "Never mind. It don't matter, really. The point is we beat you to Martin, didn't we?"

He checked the girl's ropes. "I'll leave off the gags. Even if someone is left near the beach, they'd never hear you through the storm."

Terry didn't shut the door between the rooms all the way. Outside the dark clouds choked off the last of the daylight. The palm trees snapped and twisted.

Jeff wondered why he and the girl were being separated from Grossmark. But at the same time he felt as if a load were lifted from him. He was bound tightly, too tightly to escape. But at least he was away from the kidnappers. All the time they had been in the same room his mouth had been dry from fear, fear that he might say or do something that would set them off. He had been terrified that they might get panicky or angry and start shooting.

The eerie yellow flicker of the candles in the next room helped to light the small bedroom. When Jeff's eyes became adjusted to the poor light, he could make out the girl's face. She was staring at him.

"Were you—?" she started to ask. "I mean, were you really trying to kidnap that man?"

"Good gosh, no!" Jeff said. "I—I just had the smart idea that I could take my brother's place as a driver today. So he wouldn't lose his pay. That's all. How do you figure into this? I mean, I know that you aren't in on the kidnapping with the others. But do you live here?"

"Sometimes," the girl said. "I come whenever I

can. My folks have owned the house for two years."

Jeff felt almost lighthearted at that. Her folks owned this beach house? Then they'd be close by. Maybe they were on their way here now. Help might be here, soon.

"I didn't think you were a kidnapper," the girl said. "You don't seem the criminal type, I mean. I guess this sounds weird, but I'm glad you're here with me. I was terrified before. But now—"

Jeff laughed meekly. "Yeah, I guess I understand. Misery loves company, huh? Only you have the wrong Tyler, I'm afraid. John's the take-charge one. He doesn't think I can get across town without his directions." Jeff sighed. "Maybe he's right."

"What do you think those men want from Mr. Grossmark?" the girl asked.

"If they're terrorists, I guess they want power or somebody released from prison or maybe just publicity. But they don't strike me as terrorists. They haven't been making speeches to us or anything like that. My guess is, they are plain everyday kidnappers. They probably want money and lots of it."

"But what about us?" the girl asked, her voice quavering, almost a whisper.

Jeff shut out the question.

After an agonizing silence, the girl spoke, almost cheerily. "Oh, by the way, my name is Marla, Marla Rheson."

Jeff laughed slightly. They'd known each other for what seemed like an eternity, yet they hadn't known or even cared to know each other's names until now.

"I'm Jeff," he said, shifting slightly in his chair. "Jeff Tyler. My brother's John, the guy they named in the newscast. Boy, is he going to be shocked to find out his little brother's messed up in this!

"Listen, Marla. Pretty soon your folks will send someone to look for you."

Marla dropped her chin, sighing a weary sigh.

"Marla?" Jeff said. "Marla?"

As she turned her head slightly toward him, the light from the other room glistened off a tear that hovered, ready to spill onto her cheek.

"My folks won't come," she murmured. "The truth is, they don't even know I'm here."

# CHAPTER ELEVEN

Jeff felt his heart thumping against his chest. "What do you mean?" His voice was hoarse, hollow. "What do you mean, they don't even know that you're here?"

Her lower lip trembled as she blurted out the words. "My folks are probably out of the country. They most always are. And if they aren't, they still don't know where I am. I live in San Antonio, at a private girls' school. As far as my parents are concerned, I'm at school inland, far away from the danger of Hurricane Bernice—and all this."

"Then nobody is going to miss you? What about the school officials?"

"I told them I was visiting my aunt, and I wrote down a phoney address. They'd be glad if I just disappeared. I—I'm not what you'd call your average happy, cooperative student. The truth is school seems to be just one big rule made to make my life miserable. In by ten. Up by six. Breakfast by seven. I can't stand the rules. So I break them. I guess I'm always in trouble for breaking rules."

Jeff sighed wearily. "Well, you have certainly shattered my last hope. We really are on our own then." The words echoed in his head. *On our own. On our own.*

"But they'll have to let us go, don't you think? I mean, once they have the money or whatever it is they want from that Mr. Grossmark, won't they just turn us loose?"

Jeff turned his head from her. He could feel her eyes penetrating the dark, looking to him for an answer. But the only answer he had wasn't one she'd want to hear. It wasn't one he wanted to say, to even think.

"Well, Jeff, old boy," he scolded himself silently. "You wanted independence from your brother. You got it. You don't have John to get you out of this one. Let's just see how grown-up you really are."

"Jeff?" Marla broke into his self-scolding. "You don't think they'll let us go, do you? But why have they let us live this long?"

He bit his lip, trying to figure out the answer. "I'm not sure. But I know they can't let us give their descriptions to the police. We've heard and seen too much already. Maybe they want to make it look as if we were killed by the storm.''

Marla's voice was flat, quiet—as ordinary as if she were refusing a second helping of potatoes. ''I don't want to die.''

She had to be scared, as scared as he was. And Jeff knew she was counting on him to think of something. At last, someone was looking to him for leadership. But right now he didn't feel at all like a leader.

''If I can figure on a way out of this, can I count on you to help?'' he asked.

Marla hesitated. ''I honestly don't know. I want to help, to be really brave. But I've always run from trouble. Nobody counts on me. Nobody.''

''There's nothing wrong with being scared,'' Jeff said. ''I'm scared, too. Being brave isn't being unafraid. It's doing something even though you *are* afraid, I think.''

''I—I'll do my best,'' she answered.

Jeff sighed. ''It's time for both of us to grow up—fast.'' If they didn't, they might not get the chance to grow up, he knew.

''Listen, I saw a surfboard on the porch when I got here. Is that yours?'' Jeff asked.

She nodded. "I got fed up with being jumped on at school, so I ran off and came to the beach house. I wanted to take advantage of the waves kicked up in the Gulf. When I came back in, this guy was here."

"Surfing takes plenty of nerve," Jeff said. "I think you'll be brave enough when the time comes." If I can come up with a plan, he added to himself.

The beach house shuddered in the wind. Even though they were on the leeward side, they could feel the wind growing stronger by the minute.

There was a crackling, whistling noise, then a thrumming.

Marla whispered, "The generator. They're using the ham radio. I'm sure of it."

"I wonder if they're talking to that guy who took the pictures to the mainland," Jeff said.

"Who else would they risk using the radio for?" she asked.

Through the slightly open door, Jeff could see Mr. Grossmark pacing back and forth. The oilman was talking, but Jeff couldn't understand what he was saying.

Jeff wiggled his nose. "If only my hands were loose, I could think better—and I could scratch my nose. It's killing me, it itches so!"

Marla laughed. Her face brightened for a second—long enough for Jeff to realize she was really an attractive girl. He grinned back.

In the other room the radio scratched and squawked as someone turned up the volume.

"Gale force winds are expected on the coastline around five tomorrow morning," the announcer said. "A hurricane warning is now in effect for the coastline from Matagorda Island to Gulfport, Mississippi. Gale force winds extend 100 miles out from the center of the hurricane. This is a *warning*, not a watch."

Jeff and Marla stared at each other, not speaking. A warning, not a watch. A warning meant the hurricane was on its way, for sure. And the beach house would never make it through the storm.

# CHAPTER TWELVE

The broadcast continued, spilling out warnings and precautions.

"All persons in low-lying areas are advised to evacuate and seek shelter. Flash floods and high wind damage are expected. Stay tuned to this station or NOAA weather radio, but be advised that radio communications may be cut off.

"As clocked by the reconnaissance plane, hurricane winds have risen to 120 miles an hour, with gusts up to 200 miles. It now appears that Bernice is as strong a storm as Carla.

"And now, these further developments in the case of the missing oil executive, Martin Grossmark," the announcer continued. "The single kidnapper is now believed to be sixteen-year-old Jeff Tyler, a Houston high-school student whom teachers and neighbors describe as a quiet, average student. His brother is being questioned by authorities and insists there must be a mistake.

"Photos taken of Grossmark with the kidnapper have been delivered to this studio and shown to John Tyler. He admits that the kidnapper does bear a marked resemblance to his brother.

"Shown a photograph, the manager of the convenience store on I-45 positively identifies the young man as the one who purchased supplies."

The announcer repeated the information given earlier. Then he quoted one of the cartel executives. "By prior agreement among all of the members of the oil cartel, no ransom money will be paid for any member of the cartel or his family."

Terry's voice boomed above the growling wind and the announcer's voice. "The cartel is supposed to give us the money!" he shouted. "How we going to make any money out of this if the cartel don't pay off? Just our luck to get a lousy loser. Your cartel don't even think you're worth the ransom!"

There was the distinct sound of someone being struck. Jeff heard a gasp. Then something—or someone—was slammed into the wall that divided the two rooms.

"You'll get your money! I promise!" It was the oilman's voice, and he sounded frantic, in pain. "Don't hurt me, please!"

"Yeah?" Nick yelled. "So how are we going to get the money if the cartel don't pay? Are you going to pay us?"

"I—I don't have that kind of money. The cartel is just saying that so they won't frighten the stockholders. They'll pay—really! Just wait until you hear from your other man. He'll tell you!"

"And just how are we going to hear from him? You really think he's going to contact us on that ham radio? What if he's caught?"

The voices in the other room became quieter. The radio went silent. Jeff looked at Marla.

"That settles it," he said. "The cartel might not even bargain for Mr. Grossmark. You and I don't stand any chance. We've got to get out of here."

"But how? And what about Mr. Grossmark?" Marla asked. "We can't leave him behind, can we?"

Jeff bit his lip, frowning. "We may have to. If we can just get away, we can send help. But there's no way we can get him away from Terry and Nick as long as they keep him in there with them—and the guns. The radio announcer said something about Mr. Grossmark being in Houston to answer questions about some land leases. Do you think these guys could have anything to do with that?"

"I suppose," Marla agreed. "But they don't seem to be talking about leases or land or anything. They want money—that's what they said."

Jeff let his breath out in a slow whistle. "Yeah. It just seems funny that Grossmark is kidnapped at the same time he's being called to court. But I guess Terry and Nick must be just plain kidnap-for-money types. It sounds as if they've hurt Grossmark pretty badly, too. Do you think he's all right?"

"I don't know," Marla said.

Jeff shifted in the chair. He opened and closed his hands, trying to regain circulation in them. "Something bothers me," he said. "This house had to be already picked out as a hideaway. Terry knew right where it was. It's only a coincidence that you were here—it should've been empty for the fall, right?"

Marla nodded. "And I'd sure like to know how these guys picked my house for their dirty work."

"Another thing—Nick knew right where to meet Terry and the van in the shopping center."

Marla tilted her head slightly, as if trying to comprehend Jeff's idea. "You'd expect them to have everything planned right down to the last detail, wouldn't you?"

"I guess," Jeff admitted. "But I am willing to

swear to you that we weren't being followed from the airport—I was watching. So how did the first kidnapper guess that we'd stop at that phone booth along the Eastex, unless—"

No, Jeff told himself. That would mean that Grossmark was part of his own kidnapping plan.

That would explain why the oilman wasn't tied up and why he felt free to give orders to Terry and Nick. But Martin Grossmark would have known the cartel wouldn't pay a ransom. So why would he arrange for himself to be kidnapped—kidnapped and beaten? It made no sense. The man had to be innocent.

Again they heard a muffled groan and the sound of a body being slammed against a wall.

No one would put himself through that kind of treatment on purpose, Jeff told himself. Besides, why would Grossmark pretend to be innocent in front of two kids who wouldn't be allowed to escape?

"That poor man is taking an awful beating," Marla said. "They're going to kill him."

The awful sounds from the other room finally stopped.

What if Nick and Terry had killed Grossmark? If they had, Jeff knew he and the girl would be next.

# CHAPTER THIRTEEN

"The storm is getting worse," Jeff told Marla. "It'll cover any noises we make. It's worth a try."

"What noises?" she asked. "What are we going to do?"

"We're going to get out of here. We'd better pool our resources—and quick," he said. "What do you do well? What can we use?"

Marla stared back at him. "Nothing—I don't see what you're getting at, anyway."

"Listen," Jeff snapped. "We're about to become an endangered species. What can we do to survive? What do you do that we can use to our advantage?"

Her shoulders heaved as she sighed heavily. "I won a red ribbon in swimming last year, and my hobbies are spear fishing and surfing. I can name all the songs recorded by Waylon Jennings. But mostly I'm good at making trouble, I guess," she concluded.

Jeff bit his lip thinking. "I've learned a lot of stuff about flying—ground school stuff and communications—at magnet school. But fat chance any of that will come in handy with no electricity and a storm barreling in on us. I don't swim well, but I can stay afloat. I was too weak a swimmer to take lifesaving classes or anything. But I'm fairly good at fixing cars."

"A mishmash of skills—not much escape potential between us, is there?" Marla asked. "Why can't one of us have been a magician? With a specialty in disappearing?"

"First things first," Jeff said. "We have got to get out of these ropes. I'm going to try to move my chair over to yours so we can work on each other's ropes."

Jeff leaned forward slightly, then pushed back. He pushed forward harder, then back, trying to rock his chair. Suddenly it slipped, and he tumbled to the floor.

The door flung open. Terry and Nick came in, carrying Mr. Grossmark's limp body between them. They flung him onto the bed. For a moment they did not seem to notice Jeff lying on the floor.

Terry glared at Martin Grossmark. "I should've known better," he muttered. "But we'll get our money one way or another."

Jeff wiggled slightly. His bound hands felt a sharp sting. Glass—glass from the broken window. It must have blown here from the other room. Maybe he could use it to cut his ropes.

"I should have thrown an anchor on you," Terry growled, suddenly noticing where Jeff had fallen. He roughly pulled the chair upright. Then, without saying anything more, he and Nick left the bedroom. Terry slammed the door shut.

Jeff and Marla were in total darkness now, except when forks of lightning lit the room.

"Jeff?" Marla called to him. "Jeff, are you all right?"

"I may never play the violin again," he replied.

"What?"

"Oh, never mind. Just trying to be funny. But everything's going to be okay. I managed to get a little piece of—ouch—glass off the floor. Just give me some time and I'll—oh, blast!"

"Jeff?"

"I'm okay. I'm just cutting my fingers more than the rope. I'll get the hang of it in a minute. Just keep talking to me, okay?"

"About what?"

"About what you're going to do when we get out

of here. Okay? What're you going to do, Marla?"

He could hear her soft sobs, see her head bent low. "Marla? Talk to me. Hear?"

Slowly Marla raised her eyes. Flashes of lightning reflected in them. "If we—"

"No, Marla," Jeff corrected. "Not if—when. *When,* Marla."

She snuffled. *"When* we get out of here, Jeff Tyler, I'm going to give you a great big hug. That's as far as I've thought it through."

He felt a few strands snap as the glass dug through the ropes. Jeff laughed. "And I'll give it right back!"

"Any luck?" she asked.

"A little," Jeff replied. "Can you see Mr. Grossmark? Is he alive?"

"I think he's breathing, but that's about all. They must've really knocked him out."

After what seemed like hours to Jeff, he felt the ropes give way. He massaged his bleeding fingers, feeling the needle pricks of circulation returning.

He bent forward to untie his ankles, then quickly untied Marla and rubbed her wrists until she felt her circulation return.

"All I can hear is the ham radio in the other

room," Marla whispered. "Do you think there's any chance Terry and Nick could have left?"

"No chance," Jeff said. "That room is on the Gulf side. It's getting the worst of the wind. If they're smart, they've made a shelter with the heavier furniture and are hovering against the leeward wall."

Cautiously Jeff moved to the window. He looked out, straining to see into the murky darkness.

Flimsy wooden shingles ripped off the beach house and blew past.

"If we can just drop through this window to the ground," he whispered, "we can head northeast. Maybe we can make it to the center of town, to the weather bureau. We can get help."

Jeff knew that was next to impossible. But maybe they could at least make it to a safer building, one far enough away so Terry and Nick wouldn't find them.

Lightning forked across the sky in a revealing flash. Jeff sucked in his breath, taking in the scene.

Angry waves slapped just under the window. The beach, the dunes, the van, the pillars that held up the fragile beach house—all of them were under water.

He let his breath out in a slow, whistling sigh.

"Now what?" he moaned. "How are we going to get out of here? We're trapped!"

# CHAPTER FOURTEEN

Jeff had hoped—wanted to believe—they could drop to the ground and make a run for it. Maybe even use the van to get away.

But with the currents running so dangerously swift and the waves so high, there didn't seem any way that plan could work.

Marla joined Jeff at the window.

"We'll have to swim for it," she said.

"You've got to be kidding!" he said. "Even a strong swimmer would run a risk in that surge. I know I'd never make it. You go, if you feel you can, Marla. And send back help."

"I'm not going to leave you here with those men!" she protested. "I'll help you. We can do it together. I have an idea."

Quietly she eased one of the dresser drawers out

and dumped its contents on the bed next to the unconscious Grossmark. A watertight flashlight and some linens tumbled into a pile.

Jeff tucked the flashlight into his belt. It could come in handy, no matter what happened.

"We'll tie ourselves together," Marla said. "That way we won't get separated by the current."

Jeff frowned. "I'm not a strong swimmer. I might go under. If I were tied to you I could drag you under with me," he argued. "It's too dangerous."

Marla ignored him and continued to rip the linens into strips. She tied them together, tugging to test the knots.

"You can use the dresser drawer as a float," she said. "Upside down, it should be buoyant enough. I read once that people who survived the 1900 storm here lashed themselves to furniture. Some of them were carried by the current all the way to the mainland. I think the drawers will work. We'll be carried farther inland, toward higher ground."

Jeff suddenly remembered. "Hey," he whispered. "There are life vests in the bathroom closet—I saw them when they let me in there. With one of those on, I know I wouldn't drag you under."

He glanced at Mr. Grossmark. "We could even

slip one on Mr. Grossmark. Then we wouldn't have to worry so much about keeping him afloat."

Marla sighed. "I wish we didn't have to take him with us. But Terry and Nick will kill him—they almost have already. We can't leave him."

Jeff nodded. "You're right. It would be cruel to leave him behind."

"I'll get the vests," Marla said. "I know my way around this place in the dark. We can't risk using the flashlight."

She eased away from Jeff, feeling her way in the dark around the bed toward the bathroom. Jeff kept a nervous eye on the door. He jumped when he felt Marla's cold fingers touch him. She shoved a vest into his hand.

Jeff shrugged into his vest, buckling it as snugly as he could. Marla slipped into her vest, too.

"Let's get the vest on Mr. Grossmark now," he whispered. "I'll try to lift his feet off the bed. You slip the preserver around him, okay? I think we'd better tie his briefcase to a vest, too. Otherwise it could act like an anchor and pull us all under."

Jeff's cut hands hurt. But he struggled to lift Grossmark, while Marla pulled the life preserver up around the man's body. Martin Grossmark's head jerked and rolled, and he moaned weakly. Jeff held his breath, hoping Terry and Nick wouldn't hear. The noise of the storm probably muffled the groans, but he couldn't be sure.

Marla tied another preserver to Grossmark's briefcase, then helped Jeff pull the oilman to his feet. Marla grabbed one of Mr. Grossmark's arms and slipped it around her shoulder. Together Jeff and Marla half carried, half dragged the unconscious man to the window. They slowly eased him to a sitting position on the floor, propping him against the wall.

Jeff pulled and pushed at the window. "It's stuck!" he whispered.

Marla abandoned Mr. Grossmark to help Jeff, and together the two of them managed to get the window raised as high as they could.

Cold rain whipped in. Outside, the water below looked as angry as Jeff had ever seen it.

Marla reached for the strips of linen. Jeff tied the end of one to his own waist, leaving several feet of slack. He tied the other end to Mr. Grossmark's waist. Marla tied another strip around herself and around the oilman.

"Even if we get caught in undertows, I think we

should be able to make it, with all of us tied together —don't you?" she asked. She seemed a little less confident than Jeff felt, which wasn't very confident.

She stood and looked at him, trembling.

"Marla," Jeff said, pulling her into his arms. "I just want you to know that I think you're terrific, and if we don't make it through this, I want—"

Marla placed her fingers over his lips. "Don't even think that, Jeff. We are going to make it—and I think you're pretty terrific, too." She kissed him quickly. "Now, let's play Superman and Wonder Woman and get out of this mess, okay?"

He grinned. "I think it'll take both of us to get him out the window. So let's lower Mr. Grossmark first, then we'll jump in."

Marla nodded, reaching to help pull the oilman to his feet again.

Jeff winced as he clamped his cut hands around the unconscious man. He bit his lip to keep from crying out.

He and Marla managed to get Mr. Grossmark to a near standing position. While Jeff supported him, Marla lifted the oilman's one leg up through the open window. Then Jeff supported Grossmark's entire weight while Marla shoved his other leg outside.

Jeff lifted and shoved the man forward. Now Grossmark sat unconscious on the sill, his legs dangling out the window.

"This is harder than I'd imagined," Jeff whispered. "We're going to have to slide him out the rest of the way, I guess. Keep hold of his arm, if you can, and we'll try to ease him into the water. We've got to go right after him—he's going to pull us in."

Marla climbed onto the sill beside the oilman. "I'll jump in first, then you push Grossmark out and follow yourself."

Marla took a deep breath and slipped out the window into the water. Jeff felt a sudden and wrenching jerk as the oilman tumbled after her. As fast as he could, Jeff slid out himself, yanked by the weight of Marla and Grossmark into the icy current.

At first he went under water, then he felt himself being jerked and tumbled and tossed as each wave hit.

"Marla. . ." His shout turned into a sputter as he gagged on a mouthful of salt water. Frantically, he tried again. "Marla! Are you all right?"

Above the sounds of the churning water her voice carried to him. "Yes! Is Mr. Grossmark okay? I can't see anything!"

"I can't see him, either," Jeff shouted. "But I can feel him pulling. He's still attached!"

Jeff struggled to keep his head above water. Rain battered against him. He was tossed and pulled with the angry waves, and he felt queasy, as if he was on the rollercoaster at Astroworld. Seaweed and debris slapped at his face.

Where were they? he wondered frantically. By now they should have moved inland. He forced his body against the current, to look back. If he could see the beach house, he'd know where he was.

Lightning licked across the sky. Then he saw the house. But it was not behind him, where he'd expected it to be. It was to his right. They were not moving inland. Something was wrong!

"Jeff!" Marla screamed. "Jeff, we're going in the wrong direction!"

Now Jeff remembered what he had learned about storm currents from his weather classes. In a bad storm currents traveled from left to right, not inland like regular tides.

"Ohhhhh," the oilman yelled. "Wha—" He was coming to in the icy water.

"Hang on, Mr. Grossmark!" Jeff shouted. "You're going to be okay. Just hang on!"

He prayed he was right. But with the current toss-
ing them in the direction they were going, they could
wind up missing high ground on Galveston Island
altogether. They could wind up on the mainland
eventually—if they were very lucky. Or they could
wind up in open water.

"Hang on," he shouted to the man again.
"We're going to be okay."

Jeff shook from pain and cold, or maybe fright.
He wasn't sure. He didn't care. He was still alive, but
that was all he knew.

# CHAPTER FIFTEEN

Suddenly a dark, square silhouette loomed to Jeff's left.

With one fitful, angry swell of water, his shoulder was slammed into the ground. He gasped for breath and looked for Marla and Mr. Grossmark. They, too, were grounded.

Mr. Grossmark moaned and gingerly touched his eye where he'd been hit.

"I know this place!" Marla shouted. "Jeff, I know this place! I get bait here lots of times for my dad. We've got to get into the building. Come on!" she shouted above the wind and rain. She struggled to untie her sheet ropes, then ran to the door.

"It's open!" she shouted. "It's been hit by a log and jammed open. Come on, hurry!"

Water sloshed through the door, covering the first floor of the building with about six inches. But the windows had been boarded before the owners evacuated. And the cement blocks looked sturdy enough to withstand the storm.

They had landed here just in time, Jeff thought.

There was no way he could have gone farther. He stepped inside the store, flipping on the flashlight. He turned the beam up and down the aisles of merchandise.

"This is Captain Boomer's Merchantile," Marla said, still catching her breath. "He's not really a captain. But I like him a lot. He won't mind if we use some of the stuff, I know."

"There's a second floor," Jeff said, glancing at some stairs at the rear of the store.

"It's where the family lives," Marla said. "I don't think we should go up there. But I'm sure it's okay to stay down here."

Jeff glanced at the oilman. "Are you all right?" he asked. "You still look a little groggy."

"I am," he replied. "How did we get away? Are Nick and Terry dead?"

"No sir," Jeff said. "But I think we're safe for a while. I'm sure they know we're gone by now, but the storm's too bad for them to follow. We barely made it ourselves. And we had the last of the life vests."

"I—I owe you my thanks," Mr. Grossmark said. "Those men would've killed me, I guess."

"Why don't you sit on those steps for a few minutes," Jeff suggested to the man. "Get your bearings—you took a pretty bad beating from those guys. Maybe we'd better find some candles before the battery runs low on this flashlight. And I'll look for a hacksaw or something so you can cut that case off your wrist."

Near the cash register Jeff found a flashlight with batteries in it. He switched it on and added another little beam of light to the dark room.

"Here are the candles!" Marla called. "And matches." She lit several and soon the small store seemed cheerier.

"I hate wading through this water," Marla said. "Rats and snakes might have swum in here. I'm going to look for some boots. You two should put some on, too."

"In a minute," Jeff said. "I think first I ought to block the door. The windows are boarded, but what if those guys see the light through the door? The storm can't last forever, and they are bound to start looking for us. After all, we can identify them."

"They're dangerous," Mr. Grossmark muttered from his place on the steps.

Jeff located a blanket and some nails and a hammer. He nailed the blanket to one corner of the doorframe. The wind was whipping too strongly for him to finish the job alone, so Marla sloshed through the water in her wader boots to help him.

That done, Jeff scanned the small store. "If they come for us, we'll just have to be ready. I feel sure they'll wait until the storm is over, or at least until it slows down. Meanwhile, let's look for things we can use—food, first-aid supplies. I'd like to fix up these cuts on my hands. And I don't know about you two, but I'm half starved!"

Marla took one candle and searched on the other side of the store. Jeff found some applesauce, beans, and Vienna sausage. "And here's some distilled water to mix with powdered milk if you want some cereal."

Marla brought a can-opener and a first-aid kit to the counter. "This is nice," she said. "It's got every-thing you need for the beach—sunburn ointment, snake-bite kit, bandages, everything."

Jeff grinned. "Yeah, I'm especially worried about sunburn right now."

She washed Jeff's hands with distilled water and surgical soap, then spread antiseptic over the cuts.

They ate and felt a little more relaxed. "We'd better look for something to use for weapons, just in case," Jeff advised.

Mr. Grossmark still seemed to be groggy. He

staggered to the back and sank down on the stairs. Marla and Jeff searched the store.

"A spear gun," Marla called. "Do either of you know how to work one?"

"Maybe we'd better stick to more conventional weapons like baseball bats," Jeff called back to her. He reached toward a shelf when Mr. Grossmark's hoarse cry stopped him.

"For God's sake, son, don't move! Don't speak. Don't even breathe."

His voice told Jeff that something was terribly wrong. He held his breath, although he was sure his heart pounded so loudly it could be heard by everyone.

Mr. Grossmark's face was ghostlike in the pale light.

His body frozen, Jeff flicked his eyes down in the direction the man was looking.

A snake, poised on a shelf just above the water level, was coiled for the strike.

Beads of perspiration formed on Jeff's forehead. Could snakes smell fear?

Jeff's muscles flinched involuntarily. Only a milli-second later he felt a sharp, piercing pain. The snake's fangs sank into his leg.

# CHAPTER SIXTEEN

Marla screamed. She grabbed a hoe leaning against the wall. She bounded toward where Jeff still stood frozen with fear and disbelief.

She struck at the snake again and again, screaming. The snake struck back at the hoe, recoiled, and struck again. At last the hoe's sharp blade connected just behind the reptile's head. Still Marla beat it. Her screams pierced the air.

Jeff felt detached from the scene, as if a snake had bitten someone else, not him. He spoke calmly.

"It's dead, Marla. It's dead. Stop, Marla. Please, stop."

She let the hoe fall loosely to her side. "Oh, dear heaven, Jeff. It got you. That snake got you!"

The severed pieces still writhed.

Mr. Grossmark stood at her side, his face pale in the candlelight. "Maybe it only got his trousers. Isn't that right, son?"

Words tumbled from Jeff's mouth as he tried to push the reality from his mind. "Maybe it was a spreading adder," he said. "Adders look like rattlers. You warned me, Marla, that snakes might be in here. I knew that. They come up right on the porch at home aft—"

Like a branding iron searing and scalding his leg, the pain hit him. Tears welled in his eyes, and a wave of nausea swept over him.

It was like nothing he'd felt before. Not like the time he'd fallen from the tree in the backyard and broken his wrist. Not like the time he'd had his tonsils out. It was a blind, terrifying pain that made his leg feel as if it had been shoved inside a furnace.

"Marla?" he said, his knees buckling under him.

Marla and the oilman grabbed him as his body gave way. They helped him to the check-out counter. Marla pushed away the mints and candies stacked there.

"Lie down," she commanded. "Don't move. Breathe slowly. I'll go back and look at the snake. You're probably right, it was only an adder."

But Jeff knew what kind of snake had bitten him even before Marla returned, grim-faced. Nothing but poison could be that painful. Nothing.

"I damaged the head pretty badly," she said. "But I could still see two pits near the eyes. It was definitely a pit viper—a diamond-back rattler."

Jeff struggled to push himself up. "I didn't hear a rattle. They warn you first, don't they? I—"

Marla pushed him back down. "The rattles were gone. They're easily lost. It's a rattler, all right."

"I've got to get to the hospital! I'll die!"

Tears glistened in Marla's eyes. "You know we can't get to a hospital in this storm, Jeff. We can't get out of here. I—I'll take care of you," she said. "I—I won't let you down, Jeff. I've let everybody down all my life. But I won't this time."

She took a deep breath and squared her shoulders. It was as if another person was speaking. Her voice sounded sure and strong.

"I'll need your help, Mr. Grossmark."

The oilman looked ashen. "I—my head still hurts, but—of course. What can I do?"

Jeff moaned. "I'm on fire! I can't stand it. Marla, you've got to give me something! I can't stand the pain."

To the oilman Marla spoke firmly. She seemed totally in command. "I left the first-aid kit in the back where we ate. Get it, please." She turned to

Jeff. "I've watched enough old westerns to know you have to keep calm. Your heart beats quickly when you move around and are excited. That can make the poison travel fast."

Her voice was soothing, and Jeff leaned back as she talked to him.

Mr. Grossmark returned with the kit. Marla opened it up and spread out the contents—a little scalpel, a rubber suction cup, a piece of cloth, a hypodermic needle, a vial of powder, and a flat stick that looked like a tongue depressor.

She opened the instructions. "Read them to me, Mr. Grossmark. Start at the top and don't leave anything out."

Mr. Grossmark's hands trembled as he smoothed out the instruction brochure. "It—it says the patient should be taken to a hospital if at all possible. It's dangerous if a layman gives the treatment. The patient could—die from shock."

"Now we all know there's no way to get to a hospital," Marla said. "We've got between four and six more hours of this hurricane, at least. So read on. Tell me what to do."

Jeff felt as if he were drifting above the two of them, watching what was going on.

Marla ripped his pants' leg back, while Mr. Grossmark continued reading silently.

The area around the bite was swollen and purple. Marla swallowed hard, then spoke. "What's first?"

"First, we have to see that his heart is higher than the wound," Mr. Grossmark said.

The two of them scrambled for camp blankets stacked on one of the shelves. Marla lifted Jeff's shoulders and Mr. Grossmark slid the blankets under him.

"Now what?" she asked.

Long, rolling thunder covered Mr. Grossmark's reply. When it stopped, he repeated. "It's important to slow the flow of venom. Therefore a tourniquet must be applied immediately."

"I remember that from when I cut my leg a few years ago," Marla said. Quickly she applied the cloth around Jeff's leg above the puncture. She inserted the flat stick into the binding.

Mr. Grossmark nodded, glancing grimly at Jeff. "Okay," he said. "Now, see that the tourniquet is tight enough to slow the blood flow, but not so tight it stops the flow altogether." He looked up anxiously as Marla turned the stick inside the cloth to tighten it. "It says to loosen the tourniquet for a few seconds every once in a while so you don't stop the circulation entirely.''

Marla glanced up. ''Every once in a while? What does that mean? How do they expect us to know?''

Jeff's leg was swelling rapidly and turning black and blue. It twitched uncontrollably.

He gulped for air. ''I—I can't breathe! The poison's already got to my lungs. Tell John—''

''Shhh,'' Marla said, her eyes never leaving the tourniquet. ''You can tell him yourself when all this is over. You're probably hyperventilating from fear. I did that when I hurt my leg. Breathe slowly, now. In—out. In—out. See? You're doing better already, aren't you?''

Jeff obediently followed her instructions. Marla was his only chance. He was trusting her to help him.

When he'd calmed down, Marla said, ''Now what, Mr. Grossmark? Does he drink this powder stuff, or what?''

''No,'' the oilman said, continuing to read. ''This is unreconstituted polyvalent antivenom. It is activated when mixed with distilled water.''

''I'll get the water,'' Marla said. ''Keep reading.''

She returned with the bottle of distilled water. ''Maybe I'd better read this part for myself,'' she said, taking the instructions. "You handle the tourniquet, Mr. Grossmark, and let me read this."

Jeff concentrated on breathing. In-out. In-out. Slowly, slowly.

Marla carefully opened the container of antivenom. Following the instructions, she dribbled in the distilled water until it exactly met the mark on the vial. Then she plugged the container and gently swirled it.

She took a deep breath and leaned close to Jeff's ear. "Jeff, I've got to give you this in a shot, and I've never given a shot before."

He could feel her tears touch his face. "Bear with me if I'm not as gentle as a real nurse," she said.

Jeff wanted to say something, to tell her he trusted her, but when he opened his mouth nothing came.

She smiled at him as she plunged the syringe into the vial and withdrew the liquid.

Jeff moaned. The fire in his leg was so great he didn't feel the needle when it penetrated his arm.

"Now you've got to get the poison out," Mr. Grossmark said. "The first half hour is crucial." He paused, then added. "You have to make an incision with that little blade, then use the suction cup to suck out the poison."

While Mr. Grossmark continued to loosen and tighten the tourniquet, Marla poised the tiny scalpel above the puncture, closing her eyes a moment. She breathed deeply and with determination.

"I think your thick pants may have helped some," she offered Jeff. "At least the wound doesn't seem to be as deep as it could have been."

Jeff grimaced as Marla made the incision above the wound. "Be careful, Marla. You know, the venom could enter any open wound you have. The snake doesn't have to bite you to poison you."

Marla pressed the suction cup to the incision and withdrew it, emptying it, and repeated the procedure again and again.

"I—I hope that is enough," she said at last. "Oh, how I wish this horrible storm were over. You need a doctor!"

She motioned for Mr. Grossmark to sit down. "I'll handle the tourniquet now. I'll stay with him." She slid onto the counter next to Jeff, one hand working the tourniquet, the other gently stroking his cheek.

"I—I can't stay awake," Jeff said. "I feel on fire all over. Would you tell John that I'm sorry and that I—I love him, Marla? Tell him, promise?"

102

She stroked his cheek. "You'll tell him yourself," she said. "You're exhausted from the storm and the escape and the shock to your body. It must be past midnight now, I think."

Jeff relaxed a little. Marla was right, of course. He was very tired.

"I've done a terrific job on you and you've got to get well." She smiled reassuringly at him.

"If—if something goes wrong, you did your best," Jeff mumbled, his tongue thick and dry. "Don't blame yourself, hear?"

Marla leaned forward and kissed him on his forehead. He could feel her tears on his face.

He meant to tell her that he liked her—a lot—but he couldn't make his lips form the words.

Outside Captain Boomer's Mechantile, the most powerful winds of Hurricane Bernice assaulted Galveston Island. Trees ripped out by their roots, logs that had rested on the beach for years, and even the roofs of houses swirled past the store in the ocean swell. The water inside the store rose another foot, and dead fish floated to the top, their eyes empty and unseeing.

Overhead the rain drummed mightily against the roof. It finally leaked into the upper floor, then dripped steadily into their first-floor hideaway.

The wind roared, and at times the little store sounded like the inside of a train tunnel.

Jeff felt himself being spun inside a whirlpool, on a giddy, dizzying ride to nowhere. Swirls of technicolor crossed his closed eyes and seemed to drift away, carrying him with them.

He wanted to stay awake, to be alert, to talk and talk and talk. There was so much to do, so much to say, so much life to still live. He tried to push his eyelids open, to *will* his eyes to see.

But he finally sank into an exhausted sleep.

# CHAPTER SEVENTEEN

Jeff drifted in and out of consciousness throughout the night. He thought he was on the beach, collecting sand crabs with John. His mother was beside him.

Then the pain would jolt him awake, his mother's and John's faces would fade. Instead he saw Marla, bending over him, holding a blanket over his trembling, chilled body.

"You're important to me, Jeff," she whispered. "You will be all right. You have to be all right. Please, Jeff. I'm depending on you."

Important. The word sounded musical to Jeff. He'd never felt really important to anyone before. He'd never had anyone depending on him.

He'd only been a burden, someone who had forced his older brother to accept responsibility too soon.

Important...

"There's probably some poison still inside," he heard Marla say once. "There's no way to get it all. But he got the antivenom right away. It'd be so much better if we could get him to the hospital."

"But the storm," Mr. Grossmark muttered.

"Yes, I know, the storm," Marla replied with a sigh.

Outside, debris still thumped against the concrete blocks of the store. The water sloshed against the shelves inside. But the wind gusts came farther apart. The shutters seemed to rattle less intensely than before. And the rattling paused altogether every now and then.

Gradually Jeff moved into misty consciousness. He wiggled his toes, shifting his feet slightly. They had feeling in them. He realized his breathing was easier now.

Warily he touched his fingers to his eyes and blinked.

"Jeff!" Marla cried. "Oh, Jeff!" She leaned forward to kiss his cheek. "You—you're all right."

Weakly he grinned at her. "If this is all right, I don't want to remember before." His head ached. His body felt stiff and sore. But he knew he was okay. He'd made it through the crisis.

Suddenly Marla self-consciously pushed at her hair. It hung in gritty strings. Her clothes had dried, but the salt and sand still clung.

"I must look a sight!" she moaned. "I feel sticky and awful!"

106

"I can honestly say you are the most gorgeous creature I've ever seen in my life," Jeff said, managing a grin.

She grinned back. "I bet you tell that to all the girls who save your life!"

She adjusted the blanket. "Hungry? I mean, we're right here in a store. We might as well take advantage of it, don't you think?" She paused. "I'm keeping tabs on what we've used. I'll leave a note for the owners. That'll be okay, don't you think?"

Jeff pushed himself to a sitting position, feeling slightly dizzy. New candles burned in place of the earlier stubs. A small amount of light—morning light—crept through the boarded windows.

For a moment he was startled to see he was wearing John's chauffeur's uniform — at least, what was left of it. Its knife pleats were gone, the right pant leg was ripped and bloody, and the material looked beige instead of gray.

"How long have I been out? How's the storm? Where's Grossmark?"

She nodded toward the steps. "He's over there, sleeping." She wrinkled her nose.

"What's wrong?" Jeff asked.

"Well, I don't know, exactly, but something is.

After you fell asleep, Mr. Grossmark did, too. But before he dozed off, he took everything out of his wallet—I think he wanted to dry out his papers and credit cards.

"After a while I tiptoed over there and took a look at his cards. I shouldn't have, I guess, but I was curious. He had a lot of business cards."

Marla took a deep breath. She held up a soggy white rectangle. "This is my dad's card," she said, her voice shaking. "Martin Grossmark had my father's business card in his wallet. He knows my dad."

Jeff stared at her. His head still felt light, and he struggled to focus his thoughts. There was some way everything fit together, but he could only see the pattern dimly, as if he were looking into a fogged-up mirror.

"Marla, remember when you wanted to change your jeans and Grossmark told Terry to let you? Grossmark said the beach house belonged to you. I wondered then how he was so sure about that. Now I wonder if he knew about your beach house before he was kidnapped. Maybe he talked to your father about it sometime. Maybe that's why he has your dad's card."

"Dad does work with plenty of oilmen—it's possible he met Grossmark sometime. But I told Grossmark my name last night—why didn't he say he knew my father?"

"Listen," Jeff said. "Remember how Grossmark seemed to do nothing to help himself? Remember how Terry and Nick didn't even tie him up? He just hasn't acted like a kidnap victim! And I'm wondering again how the kidnappers knew we'd stop at that phone booth along the Eastex. Maybe they were following us, but I'd been watching and I'm willing to swear they weren't. And if we weren't being followed, that could mean that Grossmark told them we'd stop there."

Jeff took a deep breath. "And if you put that all together with the idea that he knew about your beach house, that could mean he was in on his own kidnapping."

Marla touched Jeff's arm, as if pleading. "You can't mean you think that Mr. Grossmark set up his own kidnapping! Why would he do that?"

"I don't know. Maybe the answer lies in that briefcase he's got chained to his wrist. I wonder what's in it."

"Probably only the land leases, don't you think?" Marla said. "That was why he was going to this meeting in Houston in the first place—to show the leases to the board of directors. To prove the landowners had been paid and that the oil company could drill on their land.''

Now Jeff's mind felt clearer. He sat up straighter. ''I wonder if there could be anything to what those landowners say. I mean, I wonder if there could be some problem with the leases—if maybe the oil company didn't treat the owners fairly.''

''You mean you think Grossmark could owe those landowners money?''

''Well,'' Jeff continued, ''it's possible. And if he's in some kind of trouble, I can't think of a better excuse for arranging to be kidnapped. You have to admit it's quite a coincidence that the kidnapping and the problems with the leases are taking place at the same time.''

''But the beating he took!'' Marla protested. ''It was awful! Surely he didn't get himself beaten up just so he would look like the innocent victim of a kidnapping!''

Jeff rubbed his leg gingerly, thinking. ''I know it doesn't make sense. But if he couldn't produce legal leases at the cartel meeting, what better way to appear innocent than to be kidnapped? If he simply disappeared without a trace, he'd look guilty. But if he was never heard from again because he was the victim of a kidnapping, then he would seem to be innocent—the victim of foul play."

"But the hurricane!" Marla exclaimed. "Who'd plan something like this in a hurricane?"

"I don't think Bernice was part of the plan. How could it be? But—"

Marla's eyes flickered past Jeff, and she mouthed a silent "oh."

Jeff glanced back. Martin Grossmark was standing behind them, his face hard and cold, his jaw still and determined.

"You really are a clever young couple," he said. "Too bad."

# CHAPTER EIGHTEEN

There was no need to pretend that Mr. Grossmark had misunderstood. And Jeff knew he'd never convince the man he and Marla didn't know enough to be dangerous.

There was nothing to lose, Jeff decided. Maybe at least he could find out the truth about this crazy kidnapping.

"Your company wanted the leases or the money you were supposed to give the landowners. Did you think they'd pay your ransom and then you could put the stolen money back into company funds?"

Mr. Grossmark's face twisted into a sneer. "Don't be naive. The ransom money would be only a pittance compared to what I've relieved them of. The best I hoped for was that it would pay off those fools who helped me pull this vanishing act."

"You thought the company would come up with the money, in spite of the cartel's no ransom policy.

When they wouldn't, you and Terry had the falling out last night. Since there wasn't any ransom to pay them off, Terry and Nick got pretty upset."

"Someone would've recognized you eventually, Mr. Grossmark," Marla said. "How could you expect to vanish?"

Mr. Grossmark said nothing. He glanced at his watch.

Jeff cocked his head, listening. The wind was almost gone. The rain had stopped. Light streamed through the door where the blanket didn't meet the jamb.

"Your pals are going to start looking for us if they made it through the storm," Jeff said. "They're going to be mad at you about their money. And they aren't going to be too happy about us, either."

"They won't find me," Mr. Grossmark said. "And they'll keep their mouths shut about this. They're not even involved, as far as the police are concerned."

"But I am!" Jeff protested hotly. "When I tell what I know—and Marla backs me up—they'll be glad to talk. They'll want to be tried for extortion instead of kidnapping."

The oilman glanced at his watch again. "If it

weren't for this stupid hurricane, I'd—" He cocked his head, listening.

The building vibrated. A shattering clatter came nearer and nearer. What was it—a tornado? Jeff wondered. He pulled himself to his feet. The cold water covering the floor sent a chill through him. His sore leg buckled under him and he had to grab the counter to steady himself. His whole body felt stiff and painful. He forced himself to go slowly, deliberately taking deep breaths—in-out, in-out.

Marla wrapped her arm around his waist and helped him to the door. Mr. Grossmark had already run out ahead of them. He waved frantically.

Above them a yellow helicopter hovered.

"A chopper!" Jeff yelled, "It's a helicopter! It must be the Coast Guard!"

The oilman sloshed through the water ahead of them and came to the outside stairs of the building. He shouted and waved at the chopper, which turned to hover over the flat roof of the two-story building.

Clinging to Marla, Jeff stumbled with her through the cold water. They climbed the slime-covered stairs, following the oilman to the roof. The chopper landed, its rotary blades spinning.

The oilman reached it first and struggled to get in.

114

His briefcase caught on the door handle. As he struggled to pry it loose, Jeff and Marla caught up.

Marla pointed east. The high water churned as two men in a motorboat approached swiftly.

"It's Terry and Nick!" Marla shouted.

Jeff shoved Marla into the open chopper door and scrambled in after her.

The helicopter lifted from the roof and swung away. Through its window Jeff could see Terry and Nick in the motorboat, gazing angrily up at them. Terry was holding his shotgun.

Jeff turned to the pilot and for the first time noticed that he wasn't in a service uniform.

"It took you long enough," Mr. Grossmark yelled above the sound of the motor.

"I had to wait for the storm to calm down. There was no way I could pick you up last night. But listen—when you said three people, I didn't think you meant yourself and two kids," the pilot said. "This is dangerous enough without involving kids. And what about those two guys down there?"

"I think they're looters," Mr. Grossmark said. "One of them's got a rifle."

"Wait a minute!" Jeff yelled. "The Coast Guard station is back that way!"

115

The chopper was headed, not east toward the Coast Guard Station, but out above the choppy Gulf waters.

A sinking feeling came over Jeff. This must be a private chopper, part of Mr. Grossmark's escape plan. No wonder the man had kept checking his watch. And Jeff was willing to bet Grossmark had contacted the pilot on the ham radio last night.

It looked as if Grossmark planned to escape while the hurricane still had authorities occupied. But how far could he go in a chopper? And why had Mr. Grossmark let him and Marla board? He could have left them to Terry and Nick.

The chopper moved farther and farther out over the Gulf. Jeff knew that Mr. Grossmark was a desperate man now. He'd never let him and Marla tell the authorities what they knew. And with a sinking heart Jeff realized what Grossmark's plan was. What a perfect place to get rid of two witnesses —too far out in the Gulf to swim to safety.

Jeff buckled himself in and sat tensed, ready for the move that was sure to come. He glanced back at Marla, who sat next to Mr. Grossmark. Did she realize what Grossmark must be planning?

On the southern horizon thunderhead clouds

116

gathered like a herd of stampeding buffaloes. Sheet lightning painted them a musty white for an instant. Jeff peered below. The waves were kicking higher again.

He reached back and gripped Marla's arm. His throat tightened. "Marla," he whispered hoarsely. "Marla, did the storm stop once while I slept? Even for a while?"

"No," she replied. "It was steady the whole time —why?"

"You've got to turn back!" Jeff cried to the pilot. "Mr. Grossmark, tell him to turn back! We've got to get on shore!"

"What's wrong, Jeff?" Marla asked. "What's the matter with you?"

"According to the last weather report, the storm was coming directly at us. Unless it changed direction this is only the eye—just a patch of good weather in the center."

"Don't worry, son!" the pilot shouted above the motor's clatter. "It's a wide eye. We've got plenty of time."

"No, please!" Jeff yelled. "The worst wind is still to come. We could be dashed out of the sky!"

The chopper trembled in the first gusts.

# CHAPTER NINETEEN

The pilot got the chopper under control again. But there'd be more strong gusts, plenty of them. They'd get harder to fight, too. And the chopper was getting farther and farther from land.

Ahead Jeff spotted an oil rig jutting from the water. They must be headed for the rig. Men and women lived and worked on those things months at a time. It would be deserted—evacuated for the storm. And it would be complete with a chopper pad.

It would be dangerous on the rig. Wind and tidal waves might bend and topple it. But Grossmark was desperate enough to take the chance. Maybe he had already arranged for a boat to pick him up there.

If he escaped by boat from the rig there'd be no way of tracing him. He could go to Mexico, Central America, anywhere. There'd be no way to prove he was even still alive, much less that he had planned the whole scam himself.

The chopper shuddered in the wind. The pilot struggled with the controls. "Hang on, folks," he called. "It's gonna get a little rough."

Jeff knew he had nothing to lose. "Why are you doing this?" he yelled at the pilot. "You know you could lose your license by helping a criminal escape."

The pilot turned around, amazed. "What are you talking about? What criminal?"

"Shut up!" Mr. Grossmark yelled. He reached over Marla to clutch at Jeff's throat. "I said shut up!"

Jeff was still strapped to his seat. He struggled to fight off the oilman. Marla pounded on Grossmark, screaming for him to stop.

Suddenly the pilot made a deliberate turn of the chopper, slamming Mr. Grossmark back against the opposite frame.

The chopper shuddered. Jeff glanced back at the oilman.

"He's out," Marla said. "He hit his head when the chopper lurched."

"Thanks for that," Jeff said to the pilot. "I'd be a goner if you hadn't maneuvered to tumble him off me."

The pilot grinned. "You're welcome. I didn't know what he was up to—honest. But we're not out of the woods yet. We'd never beat the storm to shore. We'll have to land on the rig pad. Be ready to get out —fast.''

The helicopter lurched as the pilot hovered it over the pad. Marla crawled over the oilman's sprawled form to get nearer the door.

The chopper settled uneasily on the pad, shivering in the wind.

"Get out!'' the pilot shouted. "Hurry!''

He and Marla leaped from the chopper. Jeff scrambled out the other side. There was no time to tie the chopper. It wavered in the powerful wind. Jeff reached inside and yanked at the unconscious Mr. Grossmark.

"It's going to go over!'' the pilot shouted. "Get out of the way!''

Jeff tugged mightily at Martin Grossmark and pulled him free just before a violent gust of wind picked up the helicopter and tossed it rolling, tumbling, into the water. The blades snapped off, then the chopper started to sink into the swelling, frothy waves.

The pilot crawled to where Jeff lay panting, still clutching the oilman. The two of them dragged him across the helicopter pad, which jutted from the rig

120

like a dinner plate on an outstretched arm. They hurried down the ladder to the main deck of the rig. They were off the vulnerable chopper pad, but they were still exposed. They had to get inside.

The rain slammed at them as they made their way to a door. Just as they reached it, Martin Grossmark came to. He raised the briefcase and crashed it like a giant fist at Jeff.

Jeff ducked, and the briefcase hit the metal door jamb. The case split, and in an instant the angry wind lifted hundreds—maybe thousands—of bills and sent them fluttering into the air like a flock of frantic birds.

"No!" Martin Grossmark yelled. "No!"

Jeff spun and slammed his left fist into the oilman's chin, following with a right into his stomach.

Grossmark crumpled at his feet. Jeff scooped him up as Marla managed to shove the door open.

The pilot reached to help Jeff pull the man inside. "He's a determined sucker, isn't he?" the pilot asked, still bewildered.

The pilot—he finally introduced himself as Scat Thompson—tied up Mr. Grossmark. Marla reported a radio room next to them.

Jeff looked the radio console over. It was similar to the one he'd used in class. The signal was weak and slightly garbled, but he flipped to the emergency frequency.

He and Marla burst into grins as a garbled reply came through.

Jeff told the Coast Guard the situation. "Will you get messages to our families? Will you tell them that Jeff Tyler and Marla Rheson are all right? The rig is trembling, but it's holding up okay." He reached to squeeze Marla's hand. "And so are we," he added.

The two of them and Scat settled down to wait for Hurricane Bernice to burn itself out. There'd be no rescue until then.

"It's over," Jeff told Marla, giving her a reassuring hug. "It's really over."

Marla smiled up at him. "No, Jeff. It's just beginning."

# CHAPTER TWENTY

Overhead seagulls cried mournfully, their wings spread against the warm Gulf breeze. Sandpipers skittered back and forth, gobbling at the morsels each wave deposited on the sand.

The debris left by the hurricane had been cleared away. All along the beach, houses were again taking form. Sand fences were in place, capturing the blowing sand and forming it into dunes once again.

Lollipop-colored umbrellas dotted the beach. It was the first warm spring weekend since Hurricane Bernice had devastated the island. Marla and Jeff, their arms linked around each other's waists, strolled along the shore.

"I thought I'd never want to see Galveston

again," Jeff admitted. "But it's so peaceful and so beautiful here. It's like Bernice never happened."

Marla leaned her head against his arm as they stopped to watch children playing Frisbee. "Do you know, if it *hadn't* happened, I'd never have met you, Jeff Tyler? And I'd probably have gone on acting like a stinker, doing everything I could to drive my parents away from me, although more than anything I didn't want that."

"I know. Look at the hard time I gave John! And all he wanted to do was to take care of me, to keep what was left of our family together."

"It changed him, too, though, didn't it?" Marla asked. "I mean, you are working and everything, now."

"Well, it's work, all right. But not for money. For flying time. I gas up the planes, wash 'em, that sort of thing. Then they give me flying lessons. John feels that'll help me in my schoolwork, but won't give me any money to waste on the car." He laughed. "I guess change doesn't all happen at once, does it?"

Marla paused to pick up a sand dollar. She turned it over and over in her hand. "Do you realize this is the first time since the trial that we've actually been able to spend some time together? Ugh, I'm so glad

124

we won't have to see any of them again—that terrible Mr. Grossmark and those awful men!''

"At least their trials answered a lot of questions I couldn't figure out answers to," Jeff admitted. "I just can't get over the fact, though, that Mr. Grossmark had all that money in his briefcase and wouldn't pay off those guys with it!''

"I'm glad he didn't!" Marla said. "Once they got some money for their trouble, our lives would've meant nothing to them. Grossmark's, either. He probably figured they'd kill him if he gave them money, and they probably would have, too.''

Jeff shuddered. "You know, if we'd been killed and Grossmark had gotten away, I might have been forever branded a kidnapper—just because I thought I'd be smart and take John's place. But I'm glad it was me and not John who was kidnapped.''

Marla nodded. She suddenly laughed. "Just think of the trouble the police would have had trying to figure out what part I played!''

Jeff shook his head, remembering. "It sure shocked your father when he realized it was a casual conversation he'd had with Mr. Grossmark about his generator-operated ham radio that made your beach house the chosen hideaway.''

Marla wiggled her toes in the wet sand. "That had to have happened a year ago when Daddy sold computers to MGC. I guess Mr. Grossmark had been planning this for a long time. He and Daddy sealed a deal over lunch. Daddy just got to talking about the beach house. He didn't think anything about the questions Mr. Grossmark asked him."

Jeff picked up a shell and tossed it out into the waves. He watched it sink before he spoke. "He was a cool one, wasn't he? He crossed the landowners. He double-crossed his company. Then he ended up double double-crossing those men working for him." He laughed. "I'll never forget the expression on his face when all that money fluttered into the water."

Marla ran ahead. She leaped to catch a stray Frisbee and sailed it deftly back to the waiting children. "Well, how about his company, though! The idea, wanting all the charges dropped! Just so their stockholders wouldn't go running off scared. Can you imagine?"

Jeff laughed. "I guess they'd have found a way to hush it all up eventually—if it weren't for us!"

He spotted a familiar figure down the beach and waved. "There's John, signalling. Your folks must have the hot dogs ready."

Overhead the seagulls dived into the wind, calling. Jeff pulled Marla to him. "You were right back there on the rig, Marla," he said. "It was a beginning, wasn't it?"

He took her hand and together they ran toward their waiting families.

## About the Author

When Mary Blount Christian was in the fifth grade, her teacher had her stand up in front of the class every day after lunch and tell a continuing suspense story involving other children in the room. The young storyteller quickly learned that her audience stayed interested if the tale had lots of action.

Mrs. Christian's journalism studies at the University of Houston and her work as a free-lance newspaper reporter sharpened her ability to grab and hold readers' attention. Over the years she has come to care more for the "why" of a news story than for the plain facts, and as a result she has become devoted to the writing of fiction.

Mary Blount Christian makes creative use of contemporary events and real-life settings in her novels. Of *The Mystery of the Double Double Cross* she notes, "Houston and Galveston, Texas, where this story takes place, are real cities, and both of them have been devastated by storms and floods. But Hurricane Bernice did not happen. It is only an accumulation of memories and imagination."